While I have no doubt that seducing you would be a great pleasure, I need to focus my attention on other things right now."

Though the softly spoken words made everything inside her quiver, Lara refused to give Rowan the satisfaction of knowing it. "Do you think I would fall into your bed just because you wanted me there, Your Highness?"

"I think," he said confidently, "that you would fall into my bed because *you* wanted to be there."

Her chin lifted just a fraction. "Then you think wrong. I won't be any man's temporary amusement."

"If I believed otherwise, we'd be having this conversation in bed." He grinned. "Or maybe we wouldn't be talking at all."

Her heart was pounding wildly in her chest, but she managed to keep her voice steady. "Save the seduction routine for your bride. I'm not interested."

Available in July 2009
from Mills & Boon®
Special Edition

The Prince's Royal Dilemma

BRENDA HARLEN

MILLS & BOON®
Pure reading pleasure™

DID YOU PURCHASE THIS BOOK WITHOUT A COVER?
If you did, you should be aware it is **stolen property** as it was
reported *unsold and destroyed* by a retailer. Neither the author nor
the publisher has received any payment for this book.

*All the characters in this book have no existence outside the
imagination of the author, and have no relation whatsoever to anyone
bearing the same name or names. They are not even distantly inspired
by any individual known or unknown to the author, and all the
incidents are pure invention.*

*All Rights Reserved including the right of reproduction in whole or
in part in any form. This edition is published by arrangement with
Harlequin Enterprises II B.V./S.à.r.l. The text of this publication or
any part thereof may not be reproduced or transmitted in any form
or by any means, electronic or mechanical, including photocopying,
recording, storage in an information retrieval system, or otherwise,
without the written permission of the publisher.*

*This book is sold subject to the condition that it shall not, by way of
trade or otherwise, be lent, resold, hired out or otherwise circulated
without the prior consent of the publisher in any form of binding or
cover other than that in which it is published and without a similar
condition including this condition being imposed on the subsequent
purchaser.*

*® and ™ are trademarks owned and used by the trademark owner
and/or its licensee. Trademarks marked with ® are registered with the
United Kingdom Patent Office and/or the Office for Harmonisation
in the Internal Market and in other countries.*

*First published in Great Britain 2009
by Harlequin Mills & Boon Limited,
Eton House, 18-24 Paradise Road, Richmond, Surrey TW9 1SR*

© Brenda Harlen 2008

ISBN: 978 0 263 87054 1

23-0709

*Harlequin Mills & Boon policy is to use papers that are
natural, renewable and recyclable products and made from
wood grown in sustainable forests. The logging and
manufacturing processes conform to the legal environmental
regulations of the country of origin.*

*Printed and bound in Spain
by Litografia Rosés S.A., Barcelona*

BRENDA HARLEN

grew up in a small town surrounded by books and imaginary friends. Although she always dreamed of being a writer, she chose to follow a more traditional career path first. After two years of practising as an attorney, including an appearance in front of the Supreme Court of Canada, she gave up her "real" job to be a mum and to try her hand at writing books. Three years, five manuscripts and another baby later, she sold her first book.

Brenda lives in southern Ontario with her real-life husband/hero, two heroes-in-training and two neurotic dogs. She is still surrounded by books ("too many books," according to her children) and imaginary friends, but she also enjoys communicating with "real" people. Readers can contact Brenda by e-mail at brendaharlen@ yahoo.com.

DONCASTER LIBRARY & INFORMATION SERVICE	
30122031618545	
Bertrams	07/07/2009
	£3.19

For Neill
– my real-life prince –
with much appreciation
and all my love.

Prologue

With its pristine sand beaches and crystal-blue waters, Tesoro del Mar is truly a treasure of the Mediterranean Sea. Though small in size, it has a huge appeal to visitors from all over the world.

Lara Brennan eagerly absorbed the details from her guidebook, anxious to learn everything about the island before the plane's wheels touched down at the Port Augustine airport.

Tanis Rowlands, her best friend and traveling companion, waved a hand in front of her face to get her attention. "This is supposed to be a vacation—why are you studying that book as if there's going to be a quiz at the end of our trip?"

"I'm just amazed—by the history, the culture, even the name. Did you know that it means *treasure of the sea?*"

"Tesoro del Mar." Tanis practically sighed the words. "I know that it even sounds like a fairy-tale kingdom."

"It's not a kingdom, it's a principality." Lara pointed to a line in the book.

"What's the difference?" Tanis asked.

"It's not ruled by a king, but a prince."

Tanis's blue eyes sparkled. "The country does have some hunky princes."

Lara laughed. Though she'd only ever met Prince Julian—who was happily married to Princess Catherine—she'd seen enough tabloid photos of the other three princes to know that they were all tall, dark and almost sinfully handsome.

"We probably won't even see any of Julian's brothers," she told her friend. "Rowan is an investment banker in London, Eric is an officer in the navy, and Marcus is at school in Switzerland."

Tanis pouted. "Well, at least we get to stay in the royal palace. How old did you say it was?"

Lara consulted the book again. "It was built more than four hundred years ago."

"That is old." Tan's brow furrowed. "Did they have flush toilets back then?"

"No, but I imagine there have been some renovations done and improvements made over the years."

"And the people speak English?"

"The island was settled by both the Spanish and the French, so it is officially a bilingual country, but a majority of the residents also speak English."

She skimmed over the history of Tesoro del Mar and the reign of the Santiago family, then turned the page. The photo of the castle was spread out over two pages to better capture the majesty of soaring towers and stunning turrets, wide stone balconies and high, arched windows. As much as she was looking forward to visiting the palace, she was looking forward to visiting with the family who lived there even more.

Twice every year, Prince Julian and Princess Catherine journeyed to Kilmore, Catherine's hometown in Ireland, to visit her family. Through a distant family connection, Lara had met them there four years earlier. On that visit, the royals had been traveling without their longtime nanny, and Catherine had struggled to balance the needs of her preschooler with the impatient demands of a new baby.

The princess had seemed surprised—and relieved—that her children had taken an instant liking to Lara, who had been just as enchanted by the young royals. On each subsequent visit, Catherine had invited Lara to spend time with the family, and she'd grown close to the children and they to her.

Three weeks ago Catherine had called to request that Lara visit Tesoro del Mar and meet the newest addition to the royal family. Lara had been thrilled by the opportunity, especially when Catherine had suggested she could bring a friend to stay for two weeks.

Tanis let out an excited gasp and squeezed her arm. "There it is."

Lara shifted her gaze from the book to the window and was immediately dazzled by the view.

The photos in her guidebook didn't begin to compare to the reality—certainly they didn't show the hills as being so deep an emerald green, the beaches quite as powdery white or the sea such a sparkling sapphire.

Then she caught a glimpse of the castle, and her breath actually caught in her throat.

"I wish I could stay here forever," Tanis said.

Lara heard the longing in her friend's voice but also the acceptance. Tanis would return home at the end of their holiday. For Lara the future was less certain, because the princess had offered her more than a Mediterranean vacation—she'd offered her the chance to make this island paradise her home.

Though Lara had grown close to Catherine's family over the past few years, she could never have imagined that the princess would ask her—the illegitimate child of an unknown father—to become the caregiver of the royal children. But that was exactly what Catherine had proposed. Now Lara had two weeks in which to tour Tesoro del Mar, get reacquainted with the children and decide if she was willing to leave her old life behind and make a new one here.

Catherine had urged her to take her time, to consider all factors. But in that first breathtaking glimpse, Lara's decision was made.

She was going to stay and be the new royal nanny.

Chapter One

Four and a Half Years Later—

Three days after the state funeral for His Highness Prince Julian Edward William Santiago and Her Highness Princess Catherine Mary Santiago, Rowan was still trying to accept that his brother and sister-in-law were gone, still struggling to come to terms with their deaths. And now this.

He lifted his gaze from the legal document on the desk to his brother seated across from him. "What were they thinking?"

"Probably that arranging for guardianship of their children was nothing more than a formality," Marcus responded. "They certainly couldn't have expected that they'd die in a freak explosion on their yacht."

The outing had been planned as a family event, with Julian and Catherine's three children scheduled to join them on the water. But Alexandria and Damon had both been in bed with some kind of twenty-four-hour flu bug from which Christian had just recovered, so the nanny had stayed back with the children while the parents decided to take a few hours for a romantic getaway instead.

Rowan stared again at the document giving him legal custody of the children. His brother and sister-in-law wouldn't have filled out the paperwork without his knowledge and consent, though when he'd given it, he'd never anticipated his role as guardian becoming a reality. Now it was, and Julian's children—the future of the monarchy and the country—were in his care.

"I know you never expected—or wanted—to be in this position," Marcus said. "But are you okay with it?"

"Someone needs to fulfill the royal duties until Christian is of an age to take the throne. But am I okay with it?" He shook his head. "How can I be when the only reason I'm sitting here, in Julian's office, behind Julian's desk, is that Julian and Catherine are dead?"

His gaze shifted to the photo on the corner of the desk. It was a picture of his eldest brother with his arm around his wife, their children around them. They looked so happy together—still obviously in love after fifteen years of marriage and completely devoted to their children. Every time Rowan sat behind this desk, his eyes were drawn to that picture—to the heartbreaking image of the beautiful family that had been torn apart by tragedy.

As if sensing the direction of his thoughts, Marcus reached forward and picked up the heavy pewter frame. His youngest brother's eyes were troubled as he stared at the photo. "The whole family's been dealt a tough blow— maybe I should delay my return to Harvard, stay around here to help out in any way I can."

Rowan was adamant in his refusal. "Eric volunteered to extend his leave from the navy, too," he admitted, referring to the middle brother. "And I appreciate your offer as much as his, but there's really no need for anyone to change their plans."

"Nobody but you," Marcus noted.

But Rowan was only doing what needed to be done, as both of his brothers would do if circumstances warranted.

The Santiago family had ruled long and ruled well, and the citizens of Tesoro del Mar trusted in their monarch. As much as they had openly and genuinely mourned the passing of Julian and Catherine, they would accept Rowan's rule. And Rowan, as much as he'd never wanted to rule, understood that it was his duty even more than his right, a duty that had been impressed upon all of them from their early days in the cradle.

"The truth is, I feel more equipped to step into the role of prince regent than guardian of three young children." He stared at the photo Marcus had put back on the edge of the desk and felt the weight of the responsibility heavy in his heart. He was fond of his brother's children, of course, but after living in London for the past dozen years he didn't know them very well. And he didn't know the first thing about parenting.

Christian he could probably handle. The boy was twelve—old enough to listen to reason, already conscious of the fact that he would rule the country one day and undoubtedly capable of doing so.

Alexandria was eight, with a rebellious streak that Julian had often lamented was turning his hair prematurely gray, though there had been no disguising the pride his brother felt in his only daughter.

As for Damon, well, the only words Rowan could

think of to describe his four-year-old nephew were "hell on wheels."

"The children have a full-time nanny," Marcus reminded him.

Rowan nodded. "The nanny is just one more reason I wonder what they were thinking."

Marcus frowned. "What do you mean?"

"Don't you follow the news?"

"Not if I can help it," his brother admitted. "The stories are more often about sensationalism than journalism."

"And since she moved into the palace, Miss Brennan has given them plenty of splashy headlines."

Marcus shrugged. "She's young and sexy and has a connection to the royal family—it's hardly her fault the press feeds on things like that."

"A royal nanny should be mature and dignified."

"Like Nanny Adele?"

It was with genuine affection that he thought of the woman who had raised not only his brothers and him but his father and his aunt before them. She'd passed away at the age of ninety-three while Catherine was expecting Damon, and his brother and sister-in-law had hired Lara Brennan—a twenty-year-old redhead who was the opposite of Adele Torres in every way.

"I guarantee there were never any front-page pictures of our nanny shaking her booty in a dance club," he told his brother.

Marcus laughed at the image. "I would think not—at least not if they wanted to sell any papers."

Rowan had no doubt the pictures of the royal nanny had sold lots of papers, and that was what concerned him. "What kind of example do you think that sets for Christian and Alexandria and Damon?"

"I didn't realize she took the kids with her when she went clubbing."

Rowan should have expected such a flippant response from his brother. Marcus was another favorite subject of the press—not just locally but internationally. "You're deliberately missing my point."

"I wasn't sure you had one."

"She works for the royal family, therefore, her behavior reflects on the royal family."

"You're not honestly worried about a silly tabloid photo that faded from the news more than six months ago?"

"That picture wasn't the only one," Rowan reminded his brother.

"It's not a crime to have a good time," Marcus pointed out. "Besides, she's great with the kids."

Rowan couldn't deny that fact, especially not in that moment when childish giggles floated through the open window. Drawn by the sound, he pushed away from his desk and crossed the room to look down to the gardens below.

As he'd expected, Lara was there with Alexandria and Damon, on her hands and knees on the ground. He watched as Damon tried to climb over her back, then tumbled off in another fit of giggles. Alexandria, though four years older than her brother, was clearly enjoying the game, too, and her giggles joined his as they rolled on the grass.

But it was Lara who captured and held his attention, as she'd done from the first with her sparkling eyes and easy smile, and his fascination with the children's nanny continued to baffle and frustrate him.

"It's good to hear them laugh," Marcus said. "It's good to know that they can still find joy after everything they've been through."

Rowan moved back to the desk. "Dr. Marotta has assured me that children are amazingly resilient. I'm relieved to see that it's true—at least with respect to the younger ones. I can't get a read on anything Christian is thinking or feeling these days."

Marcus frowned as he, too, turned away from the window. "Where is the heir to the throne?"

"In the library working on lessons he missed while he was absent from school."

"He's still a child, too."

"It was his choice to get back to his studies." He glanced up at his brother, forced a smile. "As you must get back to yours."

"I will. Soon. I want to spend some more time with the kids before I go." Marcus smiled as fresh peals of laughter sounded from outside. "And maybe with Lara, too."

Rowan deliberately returned to his seat behind the desk, refusing to let himself be drawn into further discussion about the nanny. As far as he was concerned, Lara Brennan was just one more problem he'd inherited when his brother's yacht blew up, and a problem that he needed some time to consider how to deal with.

It took less time than he expected.

Only a few days after his brother had left to return to university, a new picture of the royal nanny was on the front page of the paper. This time she was on the beach, wearing nothing more than three tiny scraps of material that might have been a bikini.

She'd obviously been in the water, and her puckered nipples were clearly outlined by the clingy fabric. Her glossy lips were curved in a smile of mischief as her outstretched arms beckoned to someone beyond the frame of the picture.

The punch of lust came first—a deep ache that throbbed low in his belly and heated his blood. *Mi Dios.* She was so stunning, sensual, sexy. And he was a man, as weak and susceptible to temptation as any other.

But as a man who was also a prince, he had to hold himself to a higher standard. He had to be both selective and discreet in his personal relationships, and he especially had to rein in the primal instincts to claim and take that churned in his blood when he looked at that picture.

He shoved the paper aside.

He could curse himself for wanting her, but he couldn't deny that he did. As he couldn't deny that the obvious solution to his dilemma was to remove the source of his temptation.

While Lexi and Damon were playing in the garden, Lara was gathering their buckets and shovels for a promised trip down to the beach. Lexi hadn't been thrilled with the plan, but she hadn't protested too vehemently. Lara took that as a good sign. The little girl had been terrified of the water since learning that her parents had drowned, and she knew it would take time and patience to help her get beyond that fear.

On Saturday, before he'd had to leave to go back to law school, Marcus had gone down to the sea with them. Whether he was more in tune with the needs of his niece and nephews than the prince regent or just had more time on his hands, she appreciated his efforts to interact with the children.

And with her uncle's encouragement, Lexi had ventured close enough to the water to dip her bucket and fill the moat around her sand castle. Just the first step, but an important one. When Lara waded into the shallows and got soaked by an unexpected wave, the sound of Damon's and Lexi's exuberant giggles joining with Marcus's hearty laughter was like beautiful music to her ears.

Her only regret was that Christian hadn't been there, but maybe she could entice him to join them today. He'd shown little enjoyment in anything since his parents had been killed, and she thought it would be good for all of them to spend a few hours on the beach together.

The request to attend the prince regent's office threatened to put a crimp in Lara's plans, as well as unleashing a swarm of hyperactive butterflies in her tummy.

His Highness had never summoned her to his office before. Then again, he'd never had any reason to deal directly with her before. In fact, whenever he'd visited from London, he seemed to go out of his way to avoid her. Though he was too well-bred to express his disapproval in her presence, she knew Rowan had questioned his brother's decision to hire her to care for his children.

Four and a half years later, she had no reason to believe that his attitude toward her had changed, and though she hadn't worried about his opinion too much when Julian and Catherine were alive, their deaths changed everything. Rowan was in charge now—of the country that she'd grown so fond of, the palace that had become her home and the children whom she loved more than she'd ever imagined possible.

And because he was in charge, she worried what this summons to his office could mean.

She rubbed suddenly damp palms down the front of her shorts. Lionel, Rowan's personal secretary, turned on his heel and disappeared, obviously trusting that she understood the import of his message.

She did, of course, but the children were a different matter.

"Where are you going?" Damon demanded, wrapping his arms around one of her legs in a desperate attempt to keep her from leaving.

She brushed a hand over his soft, unruly curls and responded, "I'm going to see the prince regent."

His little brow furrowed. "Who's that?"

She smiled. "Your uncle Rowan."

"Oh." He still didn't relinquish his hold on her leg.

"But you said we were going to the beach," Lexi said.

"And hopefully we'll still have time to do that when I get back."

"I want to go now," Damon said, somehow making the statement sound like a royal command.

She had to smile. It was unlikely that Julian and Catherine's youngest son would ever have the responsibility of ruling his country, but she didn't doubt that he would be able to do so. The arrogance and charm he already exhibited were as much a part of his Santiago heritage as his blue blood and dark curls.

"Unfortunately, Prince Damon, it's the prince regent who makes the rules now and I really can't keep him waiting."

Damon's eyes filled. "I liked it better when Daddy made the rules, when Daddy and Mommy were here."

She dropped to her knees on the ground beside the little boy and took him in her arms. "I know you did, honey. And I know you miss them both so much."

"I miss them, too," Lexi said, and threw her arms around Lara's neck.

She had to blink away the tears that filled her own eyes as she hugged the young prince and princess. "You need to remember that though your daddy and mommy are gone, they will live forever in your hearts."

"I don't want them to live in my heart," Lexi said stubbornly.

"Me, neither," Damon agreed. "I want them to live in the palace."

It was easier for her to ignore a royal summons than the children's grief, and more than half an hour had passed by the time she got them settled in the nursery with some books and puzzles and knocked on the door of the prince regent's office.

He was annoyed. That much was obvious to Lara by the cool, clipped "Enter" that answered her knock before she even stepped foot inside the room. Her impression was confirmed by the grim set of his mouth and the hard stare of his dark brown eyes.

She immediately dropped into a curtsy—a ridiculous and archaic formality, she thought, made even more ridiculous by the fact that she was still wearing the old shorts and faded T-shirt she'd put on to play with the children. Julian and Catherine had both insisted that she abandon such formalities when they were behind closed doors, but Rowan had given no indication that he would tolerate bending the rules. More likely, he'd see it as a breach of protocol and reprimand her for it.

"You wished to see me, Your Highness?"

"A while ago." His gaze raked over her. "Obviously, you weren't using the time to make yourself more presentable."

She forced herself to remain silent and ignore the flutters deep in her belly. From their very first meeting, she'd been nervous around Prince Rowan—much more so than she was around any of his brothers. Part of it, she knew, was self-consciousness because of his evident disapproval. Another part, though she'd never admit it to anyone else, was that she'd fallen head over heels in lust with the solemn, scowling prince the first time she'd laid eyes on him.

It wasn't logical and it certainly wasn't smart, but there was just something about the man that stirred her blood. She didn't know why she responded that way to Rowan and not any of his brothers, but she did. Despite her imaginative fantasies, she knew he would never see her as anything other than the children's nanny and a poor choice of one, at that.

And she feared that the background that hadn't caused Julian or Catherine to raise an eyebrow wouldn't be so readily accepted by the prince regent—if he were made aware of it.

"You have a leaf in your hair." His curt statement drew her attention back to the present.

"Oh." She felt her cheeks flush as she reached up, found the offending piece of foliage and quickly crumpled it in her fist. "I came directly from the garden."

"But not immediately."

"No," she acknowledged. "Princess Alexandria and Prince Damon were distressed, and I didn't want to leave them in such a state."

"When you are summoned to my office, your wants are irrelevant."

She might have a crush on the prince, but she wasn't oblivious to the fact that he could be a royal ass at times. It seemed that this was one of those times. As the flutters in her belly became knots of apprehension, she forced herself to take a deep breath and mentally count to ten before she responded. "I beg your pardon, Your Highness, but I was under the impression that it was my job to care for the children, and that is what I was doing."

"And what were you doing when this picture was

taken?" he demanded, tossing a newspaper down on the top of his desk.

Lara's gaze dropped, her annoyance giving way to shocked embarrassment, then fury. "I was on private property," she told him. "I don't know how this could have been taken."

"There's no such thing as privacy beyond the gates of this estate," he reminded her. "You should have learned that long before now."

It would be smart, she knew, to keep her eyes down, fold her hands together and apologize for her obvious error in judgment. But she hadn't done anything wrong, and her pride refused to let her beg for his forgiveness.

"Instead, you're *again* on the front page, looking like you belong in a centerfold."

Though her face was hot with a combination of embarrassment and anger, she managed to respond evenly. "I'm flattered you think so."

His dark eyes narrowed on her. "If you think I'm amused by this, you're sorely mistaken."

"On the contrary, I wouldn't think you're amused by anything, Your Highness."

"Certainly not, less than three weeks after the deaths of the Prince and Princess of Tesoro del Mar, a picture of their nanny—" he slapped his hand down on the paper "—cavorting on the beach."

"Cavorting?" she challenged.

"Is there another explanation for this?"

A very innocent one, in fact, but he obviously wasn't prepared to listen to anything she had to say. "Ask your brother," she said instead. "He was there."

She saw a quick flicker of surprise in his eyes before they narrowed again. "Marcus?"

"Yes."

His jaw tightened. "It seems that at least two of my brothers have exhibited questionable judgment where you're concerned, and though I didn't agree with Julian's decision to hire a nanny so young and obviously inexperienced, it was his decision to make. But the children are my responsibility now, and I have to do what's best for them."

Now she did drop her gaze, so he wouldn't see the tears that filled her eyes. It was her own fault, she knew, for baiting him. But his self-righteousness grated on her and overrode her common sense. It was only thoughts of the children that enabled her to ignore both her anger and her pride. For them she would grovel, she would plead—she would do whatever was necessary.

"Whatever you think that picture means, it has nothing to do with my ability to care for the children."

"On the contrary," he said mockingly, "it has everything to do with knowing what is best for them and proves to me that your judgment is lacking."

His tone was decisive, his expression stony, and she knew that groveling and pleading would have no effect on this man. Along with the realization came a stab of pain that struck deep into her heart.

"You can pick up your severance pay from the finance office on your way out," he said.

The anger was stronger than the hurt now, and strong enough to override the reason that had held her temper in check. "Is that supposed to make everything okay? Do you really think monetary compensation would make me want to abandon the children?"

When he opened his mouth to speak, she shook her head. "Oh, that's right—what I want is irrelevant."

A muscle in his jaw tightened, but he only said, "That will be all, Miss Brennan."

She made her way to the door, brokenhearted and defeated by the knowledge that there was nothing she could do now. On the other hand, she had nothing left to lose. She paused with her hand on the knob and turned back to him.

"No, that's not all," she said. "You say you're doing this because it's best for the children, but how could you possibly know? Do you think that spending a few hours at the dinner table with them on special occasions has made you an expert on what they want or need?"

He deliberately kept his attention focused on the papers on his desk, as if she was already gone. But Lara wouldn't be dismissed so easily.

"Did you know that Christian struggles with algebra and hates scalloped potatoes? Did you know that Lexi's favorite color is orange and that she dreams of being a dancer?"

He glanced up, his eyes hard and cold, but said nothing.

"Did you know that Damon hasn't slept through the night since he heard about the explosion on the yacht?"

There, finally, just the slightest flicker of something, though she couldn't have guessed whether it was surprise or distress or annoyance. And when he spoke, it was only to say, "Are you quite finished now?"

She shook her head. It was too late to hope that he would reconsider—the prince regent wouldn't let his decisions be questioned, never mind changed—but, for the sake of the children, she needed him to understand. "They need more than a watchful eye and instruction on their royal responsibilities—they need to know that they're loved."

His jaw hardened. "You are dismissed, Miss Brennan."

The tears that she'd tried so valiantly to hold back, tears of frustration and anger and hurt, spilled onto her cheeks, but she held her head high. "And you are an arrogant, pompous ass."

Chapter Two

"You really called him that?" Tanis's grin was as wide as her eyes.

"I really did." Lara sniffled as she nodded.

She'd hardly stopped crying since she'd driven through the gates of the palace, away from the children she'd grown to love as if they were her own. The children to whom she hadn't even said goodbye.

Prince Rowan hadn't refused to let her see them, so she couldn't blame him for that. No, that responsibility was entirely her own, because she'd known she would never be able to face them without falling apart and because she didn't know how to explain to them that she was leaving— at least not without revealing Rowan's part in causing her departure. As angry as she might be with His Highness, he was the children's legal guardian and she had no right—

nor did she want—to interfere with that. But, oh, how her heart ached.

Lara figured that when a person was feeling battered and bruised, she should go home. Unfortunately, home was nearly a thousand miles away, so she'd asked the palace chauffeur to take her to Tan's house instead.

Tanis had returned to Tesoro del Mar two years after Lara had settled on the island, partly to avoid her mother's attempts to marry her off but mostly to be closer to her best friend. An art history graduate and struggling artist, she worked full-time at a local café to pay the rent and part-time at the Port Augustine Art Gallery to buy her canvases and paints and—she kept hoping—make some professional connections. In light of her busy schedule, Lara was lucky to have caught Tan at home—and grateful.

"I would have loved to be a fly on the wall for that conversation." Her friend brought a bottle of merlot and a couple of glasses to the table.

Lara knew that even if she could explain her vehement outburst, her behavior was still inexcusable. "I was just so hurt and angry."

"And understandably so." Tanis poured the wine. "You've devoted four years to that family, and he tosses you out on your butt because of a sexy photo in the paper."

She winced. "I don't even want to think about that picture. I still don't understand how it could have been taken. It was a private beach—and Lexi and Damon and Marcus were there, too."

"Telephoto lens," her friend said matter-of-factly. "Then some creative zooming and cropping and instead of a picture of the royal nanny spending a day at the beach with the kids, the photographer has a front-page sex kitten."

"Thank you so much for your support."

Tan just grinned.

Lara sipped her wine. "Do you think he can have me deported for what I said to him?"

"He's the prince regent—he could probably have you deported for jaywalking, but why would he bother?"

"Good point."

"You know," Tanis said, bringing a platter of assorted sweets to the table, "you should consider the possibility that His Royal Arrogance did you a favor."

"How's that?" she asked miserably.

"Because as long as you were working and living at the palace, you were never going to get over your infatuation with him."

Lara selected a macadamia nut brownie and bit into it. "Which is the same problem you have with your work at the art gallery."

"Now at least you're free to do what you want when you want," her friend continued, ignoring the reference to her own life. "Maybe even go out on a date every once in a while."

"You make it sound like I was locked up in the palace tower for the past four years."

"You might as well have been."

"I've been on dates," Lara said, just a little defensively.

"Have you ever gone out with the same guy more than twice?"

"What does that have to do with anything?"

"No," Tanis answered her own question. "Because you mentally compare everyone to Rowan, and what normal guy could even hope to compete with a prince?"

She couldn't deny it was true, even if the comparisons had mostly been subconscious, so she said nothing.

"You're twenty-five years old," her friend continued.

"Way too young to be thinking about marriage, in my opinion, but if you really want to have a dozen kids of your own someday, you have to stop living in a fairy-tale world and start looking for daddy prospects."

"You're right," she finally admitted.

Tan's smile was smug. "Of course I'm right. And I know just the man to make you forget all about His Royal Arrogance."

She groaned. "Please tell me you're not talking about a blind date."

"Actually, I'm not talking about a date at all, but a job." She broke a peanut butter cookie in half and popped a piece into her mouth.

"What job?" Lara asked.

"Taking care of Luke's kids."

"*Your* Luke?"

"My *boss*," her friend clarified.

Lara had met him a couple of times at the art gallery and knew a little of his basic background from Tanis. A hunky widower with twin girls, if she remembered correctly. And the object of her friend's secret affection. "I thought he had a nanny."

"He did. Until last week when she ran off with a sculptor whose work was on display at the gallery."

She managed a smile. "And you think he's desperate enough to hire a nanny fired by the royal family?"

"I know he'd be lucky to have you," Tan said loyally. "In fact, I'll give him a call right now if you're interested."

Lara was tempted to say no, to let herself dream that the prince regent would somehow realize he'd made a mistake and ask her to come back, but she knew that would never happen.

"But if you're not sure, you can take some time to think

about it," Tan continued. "You're welcome to stay here as long as you need to."

"Thanks," Lara said, grateful for the offer, though she knew she couldn't accept it. Her friend's apartment was barely big enough for one person, even without all the art supplies scattered around. "But I think starting a new job would be good. I need to move on."

"Then I'll call Luke right away." Tanis was already reaching for the phone.

Lara sipped her wine while her friend made the arrangements.

"He wanted to come over and pick you up right now," Tan said when she disconnected the call.

"I could go now," she agreed.

"No way. It's a rare occurrence for us to have the same day off and I want to go shopping."

"Shoe shopping?"

Her friend grinned. "Is there any other kind?"

"I guess a new job calls for new shoes," she agreed, but her eyes filled again with tears.

Tan touched her hand. "It will get better."

"The worst part of this whole situation is that I wasn't prepared and I should have been. I knew Prince Rowan never liked me—I just didn't realize how much he actually *dis*liked me." She swallowed. "It was almost as if he was looking for an excuse to fire me."

"That's because he's an arrogant, pompous ass," Tanis declared with such conviction that Lara had to smile.

"Married?" Rowan stared at Henri Marchand, certain the information he'd just been given couldn't possibly be true. "You must be joking."

"I'm afraid not," his political advisor and longtime

friend said solemnly. "If you don't marry within six months of your thirty-fifth birthday, you risk losing the throne."

"Can I challenge the law? Change it?"

"You could try, but it would be a difficult and time-consuming process and your birthday isn't far away."

Rowan scanned the highlighted portion of the text again, shaking his head. "Which means that I have little more than six months to find a suitable bride."

The corners of Henri's mouth curved just a little, and Rowan knew he was amused by the thought of his avowed bachelor friend finally sticking his head in the marriage noose.

"That's right, Your Highness."

"And if I refuse? Would the throne then pass to Eric?"

It was a hypothetical question, really, because he wouldn't ever ask his brother to give up the career he loved in the navy just to help him avoid a pesky little matter like marriage. And if the throne passed further down the line to Marcus—no, he couldn't even imagine it. His youngest brother was barely old enough to be responsible for himself, never mind an entire country.

"It's not that simple," Henri warned. "Because Tesoro del Mar is a cross between a hereditary and an elective monarchy, the appointment of your successor would need to be approved by the royal council."

"As mine was approved."

"Yes. Much to the annoyance of the princess royal."

Rowan frowned. "My aunt Elena objected to my appointment as prince regent?"

"When a ruler dies without an heir of legal age, his successor is to be chosen from *all* eligible members of the royal family, and your aunt thought her eldest son, Prince Michael, should have at least been considered for the position."

"And Michael is already married."

Henri nodded. "I don't know that your cousin is even interested in the position, but there's no doubt his mother wants it for him, and if you choose to ignore this legislation, she will find a way to use it against you."

Rowan folded his hands on top of his desk, not wanting to give any further indication of the frustration churning inside. He understood that it was his duty to fill the role of prince regent until his eldest nephew was of an age to take his rightful place on the throne, but he sure hadn't been thinking about marriage when he'd accepted the position. Now he was being pressured not just to find a wife but to do so within a specified time frame—or put the future of the monarchy in jeopardy.

"Okay," he said to his friend. "You're supposed to be my advisor. Advise me. How exactly am I going to pull this off?"

"With all due respect, while marriage seems to be a political necessity, the choosing of a bride should be a personal decision."

Rowan just scowled.

"You've escorted any number of beautiful women to various social events," Henri reminded him. "Surely it wouldn't take much persuasion for one of them to accept a permanent position at your side."

"Choosing a suitable companion for a state dinner or a few pleasurable hours behind closed doors is entirely different from deciding who will be not just the next princess of Tesoro del Mar but the person with whom I share the rest of my life."

"There must be someone who made an impression," Henri said. "At least one woman you couldn't stop thinking about after you'd said good-night."

Rowan tried to summon memories of the women he'd

gone out with in the past year but found his efforts diverted by the image of Lara that hovered in his mind. He couldn't remember any other woman's eyes, only her vibrant green ones—the way they softened to the shade of moss when she talked about the children or sparked like emerald fire when she was angry. He'd kissed more women than he could remember, but it was somehow the lips he hadn't had the pleasure of tasting that beckoned him—Lara's lips, soft and full and so tempting. He'd dated women with long hair—some with flowing blond tresses, others with spiraling dark curls, but all he could remember now was the way the copper of Lara's hair glinted in the sun and the way the short choppy layers emphasized her delicate bone structure and creamy ivory skin.

"Obviously, there is." Henri's comment broke through his reverie.

Rowan pushed aside the haunting image and forced himself to ignore the almost painful yearning that stirred deep in his belly. "No," he lied. "There's no one."

His friend responded by arching his brows but didn't challenge his statement. "Well, then, you better start looking. Though I'll warn that you will likely be inundated with bridal candidates as soon as the media gets wind of this, as you know they will."

He nodded, having long ago accepted the fact that every aspect of his life was subject to public scrutiny, even—or maybe especially—his choice of female companions. "You're sure there's no way around this?"

"I'm not a lawyer," Henri reminded him. "But I'd assume that the law has stood as long as it has because it is supported by the people."

Rowan nodded again. "Thank you, Henri."

He bowed and retreated to the outer office.

His friend's comment about not being a lawyer reminded Rowan that Marcus soon would be. He picked up the phone to call his brother.

Marcus Santiago was jolted from a dead sleep to wide awake on the first ring. A quick glance at the clock had his heart leaping into his throat as he grabbed for the receiver. The last time he'd received a call from home in the middle of the night, it was because his eldest brother and sister-in-law had been killed.

"What's happened now?" he demanded in a gravelly voice.

"Everyone's okay."

Marcus let out a sigh and sank back into his bed. "Then why couldn't you have waited until morning to call?"

"It is morning," Rowan told him.

"Barely."

"And I wanted to be sure to catch you before you headed off to class."

"I don't have any classes that start earlier than 10:00 a.m. *local time,*" he reminded his brother.

"I'm going to fax you some pages," Rowan said, ignoring the complaint and pushing ahead with his own agenda.

"What pages?"

"A copy of an archaic piece of legislation that somehow still happens to be in effect. I need your interpretation of it and, more importantly, I need you to figure out how I can get around it."

Now this was unexpected…and interesting. "Tell me you haven't violated Tesorian law."

"Not yet," Rowan said, then proceeded to fill his brother in on the details of his recent conversation with Henri. By the time he was finished, Marcus was hooting with laughter.

"I don't care that you find this amusing," Rowan said to him. "So long as you find me a loophole."

"Maybe instead of fighting this, you should look at it as an opportunity," his brother suggested.

"How is this anything but a disaster waiting to happen?"

"You've been thrown into the roles of prince regent and guardian of our niece and nephews, which hardly leaves you any time for a social life."

"You have enough social life for both of us," Rowan interrupted.

"You can't let one unfortunate and long-ago experience sour you on the prospect of marriage forever."

"I'm happy with my life, with the freedom to date a different woman every night of the week if I want."

While Marcus could certainly appreciate that option and did, he knew that his brother had once wanted something different—until Margot had killed those dreams.

He also knew that Rowan wouldn't want to be reminded of the ill-fated affair of which he still bore the scars, so he only said, "You used to envy Julian his luck in meeting and falling in love with Catherine."

"Turns out he wasn't so lucky after all, was he?" Rowan said bitterly.

"I'm just suggesting you could look at this legislation as an opportunity to find someone special."

"I'm not opposed to the idea of marriage—just to having it forced upon me, and within a legislated time frame, no less."

Marcus could certainly understand that. "Send me the paperwork," he said, "and I'll see what I can do."

Ten days after Miss Brennan left the palace, Rowan was still trying to convince himself that he had no reason to feel guilty. But every time he looked into Damon's tear-streaked face or saw the abject misery in Alexandria's big gold eyes, he wondered if the decision he'd made was really what was best for them. Even Christian, usually so stoic and accepting, seemed to miss the nanny. And then there was his conversation with Marcus—two days after he'd fired her—wherein his brother explained the circumstances behind the picture of Lara on the beach.

He'd made a mistake—he'd reacted emotionally instead of rationally, and without having all of the facts. But the picture had done something to him, churned up desires he hadn't even been aware of possessing. It was one thing to want a woman—he hadn't lived well into his thirty-fourth year without experiencing the pull of desire and the pleasures of making love. But Lara was the children's nanny, and he was appalled by the weakness within himself that he could want a woman who was so clearly off-limits, and want her desperately.

He'd thrown the paper in the trash, but somehow that tempting image of her was burned into his brain. He couldn't sleep at night without dreaming about her, fantasizing about that slim, sexy body wrapped around him. And when he woke in the morning, hard and aching with wanting her, he could only be grateful that she was gone—far out of the reach of temptation. But after the initial wave of relief passed, the guilt settled in—guilt that, while he might have made the decision that was right for him, he'd made it for all the wrong reasons.

Of course, the decision had been made, so there could be no going back. Damon would cease throwing temper tantrums when he realized they had no effect; Alexandria would regain her appetite; and Christian would smile again. He had to remain firm in his conviction and trust that their rebellious behavior would pass. They just needed a period of adjustment. The new nanny had only been in residence for a week, and Rowan was confident that it wouldn't be too much longer before life settled into a normal routine again—and Damon would, hopefully, settle down.

He hadn't hired Edna Harris because of her gray hair or long skirts or thick clunky shoes, but he considered those to be definite bonuses. She'd been in the business of caring for other people's children longer than he'd been alive, and she wasn't a woman he'd need to worry about going clubbing on her night off or sneaking out of the palace for a midnight rendezvous with a lover. And he definitely wouldn't be distracted by the image of her laughing eyes, smiling lips or shapely curves.

Yes, Edna Harris was the best thing for all of them, especially now that he was facing a deadline to marry. He had to focus his attention on the future and trust that his erotic dreams about Lara would fade and he'd be able to sleep again at night.

His hopes in that regard were dashed by the sharp poke of a finger in his side.

He shook off the fog of his restless slumber and pushed himself up, trying to focus through the darkness on the child standing beside his bed. "What's the matter, Alexandria?"

"Damon's throwing up again."

He scrubbed a hand over his face. "Where's Mrs. Harris?"

"In the nursery."

"Then why are you here?"

"Because you can fix him."

Rowan frowned at the note of certainty in her voice. "What do you think I can do that Mrs. Harris can't?"

"Bring Lara back."

Mierda. "You have a new nanny now," he reminded her gently.

"She doesn't know the song," Alexandria told him.

He was wide-awake now, but still not able to make sense of the conversation. "What song?"

"The one…" Her voice faltered and even in the pale moonlight, he saw the shimmer of tears that filled her eyes. But she blinked fiercely to hold them in check and tilted her chin to meet his gaze. "The one Mommy used to sing to us. The one that Lara sings when we have bad dreams."

Rowan squinted at the clock beside the bed. It was three o'clock in the morning and he had a 7:00 a.m. meeting with the minister of state, but he somehow knew that his handling of this crisis could have more immediate and long-lasting repercussions than anything he discussed with Lorenzo over breakfast.

"Damon's been throwing up every night since Lara went away," she told him.

He frowned. "What do you mean—every night?"

"Mrs. Harris didn't tell you?"

"No," he admitted.

She sighed dramatically. "Damon's been having night-mares since Mommy and Daddy died. Lara used to sing to him, but now she's gone and he just screams and cries until he makes himself sick."

Rowan pulled his robe out of the closet. "Miss Brennan has been gone for ten days."

Alexandria nodded.

"Are you telling me that your brother has been waking up every night for the past week and a half?"

"Every night since Mommy and Daddy died," she said again. "But he's only been throwing up since Lara went away."

The realization that no one had bothered to tell him about this was making *him* feel ill. "Let's go see your brother, then I'll call Dr. Marotta."

Despite Mrs. Harris's entreaties, Alexandria refused to leave her brother's side, and Rowan didn't have the heart to force her. Instead, he encouraged the nanny to turn in, promising that he would wait for the doctor, then see to his niece himself. The woman pursed her thin lips in obvious disapproval but acceded to his wishes.

Dr. Marotta arrived within thirty minutes of Rowan's call. Unfortunately, he had no magical cure for the little boy, though he did give the child a mild sedative to help him settle. When Damon was asleep again, Rowan took Alexandria to her own room.

It was rare for him to be home without guests or other obligations when it was time for the children to go to bed, so he wasn't accustomed to sharing in the nighttime ritual. But as he helped the young princess into her bed and pulled the covers up under her chin, he found comfort in the routine—and sorrow in the knowledge that it should have been his brother tucking her in. He would give anything to bring Julian and Catherine back for their children, but not even a prince had that kind of power.

"Good night, little princess."

Her eyes were already closing. "G'night."

On impulse he touched his lips to her forehead and saw her lips curve in response to the gesture.

He was at the door when she spoke again.

"You'll get Lara to come back, won't you, Uncle Rowan?"

His fingers tightened on the knob. "I'll talk to her."

It was the most he could promise, but it was enough for his niece, who smiled again as she drifted into sleep.

Dr. Marotta was waiting for Rowan when he exited her room.

"Thanks for coming out tonight, Doctor."

The old man inclined his head. "It's an honor and a privilege to serve the royal family, Your Highness."

He managed a weary smile as he moved down the hall. "Even when you get called away from your bed at four o'clock in the morning?"

"Always."

He led the way to the library and dropped gratefully into a butter-soft leather chair. "What can you tell me about Damon?"

"Probably nothing that you don't already know," the doctor said. "He's had a lot of upheaval in his life over the past few weeks. He's confused and upset and he's grieving."

"What can I do?"

"Just be there for him." But he frowned, as another thought occurred to him. "I spoke to Miss Brennan about this a couple of weeks ago, and she gave me the impression that these incidents were decreasing in both frequency and intensity. Maybe I should speak with her again, to inquire if something may have happened to cause a relapse."

"The children have a new nanny now," Rowan told him.

"Oh."

It was all he said—a single syllable—and yet Rowan sensed his unspoken disapproval. Or maybe it was the weight of his own guilt that chafed at him.

Though he suspected he wouldn't like the doctor's answer, he had to ask the question, "Do you think it was a mistake to replace Miss Brennan?"

"I wouldn't presume to advise you, Your Highness."

"Even if I'm asking for your advice?" Rowan said.

The doctor considered his words. "What I can tell you

is that Miss Brennan has been caring for the children for the past several years. Having just lost their parents, they would naturally be resistant to any other major changes in their lives."

Rowan nodded and thanked him again.

As he headed back to his own room, he thought about Lexi's plea for him to fix the situation—to bring Lara back. He wasn't sure that he could, or even if he should.

He was the prince regent now, and as a leader, he had to be decisive and he had to stand behind his decisions. He shouldn't let a child's tearful pleas or the memories of the nanny's impassioned speech create doubts in his mind. He had to do what was best for the children, to ensure they got the guidance and discipline they needed.

Do you think that spending a few hours at the dinner table with them on special occasions has made you an expert on what they want or need?

Even as Lara's words echoed in his mind, he knew that the situation with Damon clearly proved he was not.

He'd done what was necessary for his own peace of mind, and he'd used his concerns about the children to justify his actions. It didn't matter that he'd truly believed he was doing what was best for all of them—he should have remembered about good intentions and the road to hell.

Tomorrow he would walk straight down that road and face a woman who could tempt him to sin more easily than the devil himself.

Chapter Three

Lara tiptoed toward the doorway of the room that Marci and Kayla shared to check on them one last time before heading off to her own bed, as she'd always done with Christian, Lexi and Damon.

The thought came automatically, as so many thoughts and memories of the Santiago children did, and was accompanied by a sharp pang of longing. She rubbed a hand over her chest, as if the action might assuage the ache in her heart. She knew there would come a time when she would think of them with fondness and without pain, but she feared that time was a long way in the future.

Pushing open the door of the girls' bedroom, she saw that Marci's bed was empty. Her heart jolted, then settled when she noted the two heads snuggled close together on Kayla's pillow.

She wondered if one of the girls had had a bad dream

or if they sometimes just preferred the comfort of sleeping close together. She'd have to ask Luke. After more than a week with his family, she was still getting to know them, learning their routines, discovering their likes and dislikes.

The twins had accepted the news that she was to be their new nanny easily, if not warmly. They were quiet children, polite and well mannered. Certainly they'd given her no trouble, nor had they given any indication that they wanted or needed her presence in their lives.

Luke, at least, seemed grateful to have her around. The widowed father never failed to notice the little things she did—the fresh flowers in the parlor, the tidying of the books in the library, the weeding of the flowerbeds out front—and he was always appreciative of the simple meals she prepared. Though cleaning and cooking hadn't been part of her responsibilities at the palace, she was grateful for the additional tasks now because they helped her feel as if she was making a real contribution.

As she turned away from the girls' bedroom, she found herself thinking again of Julian and Catherine's children. She wondered if their new nanny checked on them at night, if she made sure Christian had turned out his light before falling asleep, if she gently brushed Lexi's hair away from her face, if she tucked Damon's covers around him. And she wondered—and worried—who was comforting Damon when he awakened in the night.

Not Prince Rowan, she was certain. His rooms were on the fourth floor of the palace, and the nursery was two stories below. But maybe Damon's nightmares had finally stopped. For his sake, she hoped so, though she suspected that it would take some time still before he accepted the loss of his parents and managed to sleep without dreaming of them.

She was pulling back the covers to climb into her own

bed when she heard a knock at the door. She frowned and glanced at the clock on her bedside table as the knock sounded again. It was almost eleven, and though she was hesitant to answer the door at such a late hour, she was even more reluctant to have the girls awakened by the pounding.

And it was a pounding now, as whoever was at the door was obviously growing impatient.

She grabbed her robe from the back of the chair and shoved her arms into the sleeves, reaching the bottom of the stairs just as the door of Luke's office swung open. The disheveled hair and creases on his cheek confirmed that he'd fallen asleep at his desk again.

"I've got it," he said.

Lara hovered behind him, her curiosity turning to shock when he opened the door and she saw who was standing on the porch.

But Luke clearly didn't recognize the prince, because the furrow in his brow deepened. "Can I help you?"

"I need to speak with Miss Brennan." Rowan's gaze moved past Luke to settle on her.

She was suddenly conscious of the way she was dressed—or rather *not* dressed—as she automatically dropped into a curtsy. "Your Highness," she murmured.

"Your Highness?" Luke echoed, immediately stepping away from the door and offering an awkward bow. "Forgive me, I didn't realize—"

"It's all right," the prince said, interrupting. "I'm the one who should apologize for intruding at such a late hour. I wanted to come sooner but got held up at dinner with the Japanese ambassador."

His eyes again shifted from Luke to Lara, narrowing as he took in her employer's rumpled appearance and her nightclothes. His jaw tightened, but he made no remark.

He didn't need to. She knew what he was thinking, because she knew he'd always had a less-than-favorable opinion of her, and she didn't care. Not anymore.

She lifted her chin. "Why are you here, Your Highness?"

His eyes lifted to hers, and the intensity in that dark gaze sent a jolt of heat straight through her. Then he spoke the words she'd never thought she'd hear him say, four words she was helpless to resist.

"Because I need you."

There were any number of people Rowan could have sent from the palace with his inquiry, but he knew that passing off the task would have been cowardly. He needed to see Lara—Miss Brennan—himself, to apologize to her personally and to make his appeal directly. It was the only way he could be sure that she wouldn't refuse.

She didn't owe him anything. He was all too aware of that fact. Just as he was aware that she would want to turn down his request. He had enough of both pride and stubbornness to recognize those qualities in someone else. He also recognized weakness, and he knew Lara Brennan had three: Christian, Alexandria and Damon. Yes, she would want to turn him away, but she wouldn't refuse the children anything.

The man who answered the door—her new employer? her lover? Rowan pretended it didn't matter—excused himself so the prince could speak with Lara in private.

She led him into the kitchen and gestured for him to sit, though she didn't take a seat herself. Instead she tightened the belt on her robe and turned away from him to make a pot of tea.

He could have told her that he didn't want any damn tea, but he knew that what he wanted wasn't really important right now. And she seemed to need to do something to keep herself busy while she considered the implications of his appearance on the doorstep.

She set the kettle on the stove and flicked a knob to turn on the burner before she faced him again. "Why do *you* need *me?*"

One corner of his mouth lifted in response to her blatant skepticism. "I suppose I can't blame you for being doubtful. And the truth is, I considered every other option before I came here tonight."

"How did you know where to find me?" she demanded.

"Your friend, Tanis—the one you went to see the day you left the palace." The chauffeur had given him the address to which he'd taken her, though getting further information from her friend had proven quite a bit more difficult.

"You mean the day you fired me?"

"I wouldn't have thought you were the type to hold a grudge, Miss Brennan."

"But you really don't know anything about me, do you, Your Highness?"

"You're right," he agreed. "But I'm hopeful that you won't let your animosity toward me prevent you from helping a child."

"Who is it? What's wrong?"

This immediate reaction confirmed his assessment of her character. "It's Damon," he told her. "He's been having nightmares."

Her tension visibly leaked away. "He's been having nightmares since his parents died."

"I know." He looked away. "I mean, I know *now,* but I didn't realize how bad they were."

She didn't say anything.

"Dr. Marotta said they'd been getting better, that you were helping Damon deal with the loss."

"I don't know that anything can really help."

"You can," he insisted.

She just shook her head.

"It's not just Damon's nightmares," he continued. "Alexandria is hardly eating and Christian barely speaks without the words having to be pried out of him."

"What do you think I can do?"

"You could come back," he said.

"No." She turned away from him again, but not before he saw the shimmer of tears that filled her eyes.

"Just like that? You won't even think about it?"

"I have another job now."

"The man who answered the door—"

"Luke Kerrigan," she told him.

"You work for him?"

"What did you think, that I'm just here to sleep with him?"

He knew she was baiting him, and still the thought filled him with inexplicable fury. While she switched off the burner beneath the whistling kettle, he took a deep breath, forced his hands to unclench and calmly said, "I'll talk to Mr. Kerrigan. I'm sure we can come to some kind of arrangement."

"You mean you're going to pull rank."

"I'm going to do what's best for my brother's children."

"What about Luke's children?"

"I'm sure they'll miss you," he said solicitously. "But I doubt that they've formed the same kind of attachment to you in a week and a half that my niece and nephews have in the past four years."

Lara was tempted to laugh, but she was afraid that if she gave in to the emotions that were swirling inside her, tears and rage wouldn't be far behind. "Am I supposed to thank you for finally acknowledging that fact?"

"No," he said. "I don't expect you to thank me at all. But I do expect that my visit has raised questions in your mind and that you'll want to come back to the palace to at least check on the children."

"You're wrong. I don't want to come back to the palace."

She pulled cups and saucers from the cupboard, mindless of the delicacy of the china as she banged them together. So much for keeping a rein on her emotions. But honestly, the prince seemed to have an innate talent for pushing her buttons, and his unapologetic manipulation infuriated her. Though at least some of her anger was directed at herself for being tempted by his offer.

Why would she even consider what he was asking?

She wouldn't. She couldn't.

And she was going to tell him just that.

She hadn't heard him get up but when she whirled around to face him again, he was standing directly in front of her. She chose not to step back—she wouldn't retreat again.

"I don't want to return," she repeated. "And you have no right to come here now and ask this of me."

"I know," he admitted, and touched his hand to her arm. "I'm asking anyway."

It was little more than a stroke of his fingers against flannel, but she felt the heat of the contact sizzle through her veins. She would have thought, after the way he'd treated her, she'd have gotten over her silly infatuation. But all it took was a simple touch, and she was in danger of melting in a puddle at his feet.

Then she glanced up and found his gaze locked on her,

and all the air seemed to back up in her lungs as her heart pounded furiously inside her chest. There were flecks of gold in his eyes. She'd never noticed that before. Had never been close enough to him to notice. And though she knew she shouldn't be this close to him now, she couldn't seem to move away.

It wasn't until the prince dropped his hand that she managed to breathe again. And she knew that Tanis was right—Lara was never going to fall in love with anyone else so long as her heart remained enamored of Prince Rowan.

She swallowed and took a step back. "I can't."

But her shaky whisper was drowned out by the ring of his cell phone. With a quick apology, Rowan pulled the instrument out of his pocket and connected the call.

Lara was reaching for the teapot when he held his cell toward her. She glanced up at him questioningly, warily.

"It's Alexandria."

She took the phone, cursing herself again when the brush of their fingertips made her heart skip and her knees quiver. "Lexi?"

"Lara!" The joy in the child's voice was unmistakable. "I know Uncle Rowan promised to talk to you, but I wasn't sure that he would do it today. Are you really coming back? Tonight? We've missed you so much, Lara. Damon woke up screaming again but settled down when I told him you were coming home. He'll try to be really good if you come back. We all will."

As she listened to the little girl ramble on, panic and love warred inside of her. After having her heart ripped out once already, how could she possibly go back to them? How could she not?

"Mrs. Harris came the day after you went away," Lexi continued. "But she's really old and she wears ugly clothes and she never smiles. Christian said she was probably around when there were still dinosaurs, and I know that was like a billion years ago."

Lara wasn't surprised that Rowan had hired another nanny, but it was a balm to her bruised ego that the children hadn't shifted their allegiance so easily.

"She makes us do lessons *all* the time. We hardly ever get to play in the garden anymore 'cause she makes me wear dresses so that I'll learn to be a proper lady. But I'd rather be like you, Lara," the little girl said loyally. "'Cause you're pretty and fun."

Though the backhanded compliment made her smile, Lara couldn't help but wonder if she had given the children too much latitude while they were in her care. But it seemed to her that they had so little time to actually be children and the rest of their lives to be royal.

Pushing aside both yearning and regret, she finally managed to end the conversation without making any promises and handed the phone back to Rowan.

"Did you give her permission to stay up past her bedtime to make that call?" she asked him.

"I didn't set it up," he said. "But the truth is, if I'd thought it would sway your opinion, I might have."

"I wouldn't have guessed you were the type to fight dirty, Your Highness."

"But you really don't know anything about me, do you, Miss Brennan? Because if you did, you'd know that when I must fight, I fight to win."

She poured the tea, though she knew neither of them was going to sit and drink it. "If I agree to go back with you, I need some assurance that you aren't going to change your mind again." As she feared he might do after he found out the truth about her background.

"You have my word."

"I don't want your word—I want a contract."

Rowan wasn't accustomed to being challenged, and he certainly wasn't used to having his word questioned.

He took a moment to pretend to consider her request, though the truth was, he would have promised her almost anything to secure her agreement to return to the palace. But when she swept her tongue over her lips—moistening them, tempting him—he hesitated, wondering again about the wisdom of acquiescence. The children needed Lara. He had finally, reluctantly, acknowledged that fact. But he needed to find a wife, and having Lara back at the palace could be a major roadblock in that path.

"A legal agreement would help clarify our respective expectations," she pointed out.

He nodded, because he couldn't renege on his promise to Lexi any more than he could renege on the promise he'd made to Julian and Catherine to raise their children as they would have done. "I'll put my attorneys on it first thing in the morning."

"Thank you."

She still insisted on speaking with Luke before she would go anywhere with Rowan, to ensure the other man would be able to manage without her while he interviewed for her replacement. Rowan finally offered to send Edna Harris to the Kerrigan residence, figuring it was the least he could do for the nanny whose services would no longer be needed and the man who was being left in the lurch.

But his thoughts were focused exclusively on Lara as he led her out to his black Mercedes SUV and opened the passenger door for her. He caught a whiff of her scent—

something both subtle and sexy—as she moved past him to climb into the vehicle.

He felt the now-familiar and always-frustrating ache low in his belly and knew that living in close proximity to this woman was going to slowly drive him out of his mind.

She barely said two words to him throughout the journey back to the palace, but he hadn't expected that she would. He'd once thought her quiet demeanor was an indication of a docile nature. He now knew better. She had spirit and courage, and he found himself admiring those qualities as much as he worried about them.

He wasn't usually so far off in his assessments of people, but he'd made some major miscalculations where the young nanny was concerned. She was a woman of strength and depth, warmth and compassion. She was obviously devoted to his niece and nephews and clearly not intimidated by his title or status.

He knew he should be pleased. He'd gone out tonight with the express purpose of bringing Lara back to the palace, and he'd got what he wanted. So why was he so uneasy?

He glanced over at her, noting the softly faded jeans that hugged her hips and the pale-yellow sweater that clung enticingly to the gentle swell of her breasts. She hadn't put any makeup on, but her natural features didn't need any artificial enhancement. Her deep green eyes were framed by thick lashes, her cheekbones were high and sharp, her lips full and soft. She was more beautiful than any woman he'd ever known, and more tempting than any woman should have a right to be.

He tightened his hands around the steering wheel and forced his attention back to the road.

He might have thought he'd got what he wanted, but the truth was that he wanted so much more.

* * *

Lara exhaled a silent sigh as Rowan signaled to the guard in the security hut beside the tall iron gates and started up the long, winding drive toward the palace.

To a naive young woman venturing away from her home for the first time on her own, it had been like a fantasy. Four and a half years later, the sight of those impressive columns and elaborate cornices still took her breath away.

Rowan parked in front of the steps that led to the main entrance, and Lara opened her door and climbed out before he could come around to help her. She wasn't a guest; she was a servant. And whatever she might think she'd seen in his eyes when he'd been standing so close to her in Luke's kitchen, she couldn't let herself forget that.

Maybe he did desire her. And maybe it surprised her to realize he could and did. He'd always seemed so serious and disapproving, more likely to scowl at her than smile—which was probably a good thing, considering how everything inside her went to mush when he smiled. But she wasn't so innocent as to believe that *wanting* equaled *liking,* and she wasn't going to make the mistake of weaving any fantasies around a man who clearly thought so little of her.

She followed him through the front door, nerves jumping in her belly as she glanced around the spacious foyer. She'd never expected to come back, and now that she had, she was as overwhelmed as she'd been the first time. It was more than the glossy marble floors and the chandeliers that dripped with crystal, more than the heirloom rugs that muffled her footsteps and the sweet scent of fresh flowers that spilled out of enormous urns. It was a sense of homecoming, a feeling of complete happiness that she wasn't sure she'd ever known before.

He passed her suitcases to Hannah, whose warm smile reassured Lara that the housekeeping supervisor wasn't annoyed at being summoned from her bed to help get the young nanny settled back in.

"I know you're probably tired," Rowan said to Lara when Hannah had gone, "but I'd appreciate a few more minutes of your time."

"Of course," she agreed.

"We never did have the tea you made earlier," he noted, leading her into the parlor. "Would you like me to call for some now?"

"Not for me, thank you."

He crossed to the camelback settee, as if he was going to sit. Then apparently changed his mind, because he moved back toward her again.

"I don't like to make mistakes," he finally said. "But I believe in accepting responsibility for my actions. And the fact is, I owe you an apology.

"Marcus explained the circumstances behind the picture in the paper," he continued. "About your efforts to help Lexi get over her fear of the water. I wish you'd told me yourself."

"Would it have made any difference?"

"I like to think so, but…I honestly don't know. I thought I was doing what was right. I didn't think you were what the children needed. I was wrong."

He lifted his eyes to hers, and she felt those familiar and frustrating shivers chase down her spine again. Just a look—and she was ready to melt. But she refused to let him see the effect he had on her.

Instead she stiffened her spine and lifted her chin. "Is this where I'm supposed to apologize for the things I said as well, Your Highness?"

Rowan couldn't help but smile at the fierce thrust of her chin and the determined glint in her eye. She was like a warrior ready to do battle, and he marveled that he'd never before realized she was as much steel as silk.

"The circumstances being what they were, Miss Brennan, no, I neither expect nor want an apology. I do, however, hope that your opinion of me will change over time."

"You put the children's needs before your own wishes when you came to see me tonight," she said. "That's a start."

"Well, I'm going to try for some extra points by adding gratitude to my apology. I know you didn't have to come back, but I'm thankful that you did."

"I came for the children."

"I know. I'm grateful, anyway." He moved decisively toward the door. "I'll walk you up."

"I know the way."

"Of course you do," he agreed, falling into step beside her.

She frowned but made no further protest as he accompanied her up the stairs and down the hall to her rooms. When he stopped in front of her door and turned, she was close enough to touch, and he was unable to resist.

Maybe it was a test—to see if the jolt he'd felt earlier had been real. Maybe it was a weakness—a simple human need to connect with another being. Maybe it was a desire—too long denied and too strong to be ignored.

Whatever the reason, he lifted a hand and gently brushed his knuckles down her cheek. Her eyes widened, her breath caught, and he knew that the spark of awareness was both real and reciprocal.

But he let his hand drop away, understanding that to fan the flames of the simmering attraction could also be dangerous for both of them.

"Good night, Miss Brennan."

She swallowed. "Good night, Your Highness."

He watched as she slipped into her room, listened to the soft click of the door as it closed behind her. As he made his way to his own room, he worried that he'd just made another mistake, though he wasn't certain if it was in touching her…or walking away.

Chapter Four

Elena Marissa Santiago Leandres had plenty of reasons to feel disgruntled.

As the second child born to His Royal Highness Prince Emmanuel Augustine Santiago and Princess Graciela Marissa Santiago, and a daughter, she had never been considered for the throne. It hadn't bothered her when she was younger because she'd known she had a lot more freedom than her brother, Eduardo, who was constantly being instructed in one or another of his royal duties. No, it hadn't bothered her at all until she'd realized that her parents expected great things of Eduardo and all they expected of her was that she would marry well.

She defied them by running off with a farmer.

It took Prince Emmanuel a few years to overcome his fury and realize that his daughter did love the man she'd married. When he did, he forgave her impetuousness, granted her the title princess royal, and gave her and her husband a small estate on the northeastern coast of the island.

When Emmanuel died, Eduardo took his place on the throne, as was customary. Then Eduardo passed on, and his eldest son, Julian, succeeded him. Elena had accepted that without question, too.

But now Julian was gone, and without an heir of legal age to assume the crown, it had passed—albeit temporarily—to Eduardo's second-born son. Rowan's position as prince regent had been automatically approved by the Royal Council of the Throne, and she did have issue with that.

Julian's successor should have been chosen from *all* eligible members of the royal family—of which her children were a part. Their name might not be Santiago, but their blood was as blue as that of their cousins who lived in the royal palace on the hill.

There was little that could be done now, since the council had ratified Rowan's appointment and refused to correct their mistake. But if, for some reason, the current prince regent was found ineligible or unsuitable to continue in that position, Michael and Cameron would be given equal consideration with Eduardo's other children.

The princess royal would make certain of that.

Lara settled back into her routine with the children so quickly and easily she almost forgot she'd ever been away from the palace. She continued to coax Lexi toward the water, understanding how important it was for the child to conquer her fear when she lived on an island in the middle of a sea. She responded to Damon's heart-wrenching screams when they awoke her in the middle of the night, and prayed those terror-filled dreams would soon start to fade. But it was Christian who worried her most, because he gave no outward indication of the grief she knew had to be tearing him up inside. Instead he seemed to have focused his attention inward, doing everything he could to mold himself into his father's image with little consideration for the boy he still was.

As for Rowan—whether he was deliberately keeping his distance or was simply preoccupied with his new duties, their paths rarely crossed. There were no more heated glances from the handsome prince because she seldom saw him anymore, and no more fiery sparks when he touched her because he was never close enough to do so. As one week turned into two, she found herself wondering if she'd fabricated the connection she'd felt between them. By the end of that second week, she was certain she had.

It was Tuesday morning of the third week that she'd received his note. She'd been sitting by the fountain in the garden, enjoying the fresh air and sunshine while the children were at school when Lionel delivered the prince regent's message to her:

"7:00 p.m. dinner—the family dining room."

She'd frowned at the arrogant demand spelled out in his bold masculine script, because there was no doubt that's what it was. It wasn't an invitation or a request but a royal command.

As she dressed for dinner, she was still irritated by the assumption in Rowan's note that she would appear at the designated time simply because it was what he wanted. And of course she would. Because he was the prince and she had no right or reason to refuse.

Yes, she was irritated with the prince—and annoyed with herself that there could be flutters of excitement in her belly at the thought of seeing a man who had such little regard for her. But it was the same whenever she was near the prince: his status as a royal made her nervous; his presence as a man made her yearn. Maybe she'd imagined that he could be attracted to her, but there was no denying her own feelings. She could only be grateful that he seemed oblivious to the effect he had on her.

She took her time deciding what to wear, wanting something that was formal enough without being too formal. After she dressed, she darkened her lashes with mascara and slicked some gloss on her lips, then picked up a bottle of her favorite perfume but set it back down again without spritzing any of the scent. There was no point in primping for a man who wouldn't even notice, never mind appreciate, the effort. No—the prince regent would only notice if she was late, and she was going to be just that if she didn't hurry.

There were three dining rooms in the palace: the royal banquet hall could seat more than one hundred guests for state dinners and other special events; the formal dining room for gatherings of up to forty friends and family members; and the family dining room for more intimate meals. Tonight there were five places set at the antique walnut table that could seat up to twenty.

As Rowan glanced around at those five settings, he acknowledged that he'd made little progress in getting to know the children in the time that had passed since Julian's and Catherine's deaths. And to be honest, he'd made little effort to do so. He'd focused instead on business and politics, confident in his abilities in those areas, while the children remained a mystery to him.

Still, he didn't usually neglect his responsibilities, and

when he realized he'd been doing so, he decided sharing a meal with his niece and nephews could start to change the situation. He'd hesitated to include the nanny, but in the end had decided her presence might help smooth over any awkwardness with the children. He figured that would be a fair trade against the discomfiting awareness he felt whenever she was around.

The sound of pounding footsteps in the hall drew his attention back to the present, followed by a hushed reprimand, then slower and quieter steps approached the doorway. Lexi bounded in first, eyes sparkling and cheeks glowing with barely restrained enthusiasm, tugging the hand of her little brother. Damon lagged a few steps behind only by virtue of the fact that his legs were shorter than his sister's. Then came Christian, typically more serious and reserved than either of his younger siblings, and finally Lara.

Though he greeted each of the children in turn, it was the nanny who caught and held his attention—as she seemed to do whenever she walked into a room. Tonight she was wearing a halter-style dress that bared her shoulders, nipped in at her narrow waist and finished with a flirty little ruffled skirt at her knees. Her legs were bare and tanned, her feet tucked into sexy sandals that added close to three inches to her five-foot, seven-inch frame and revealed toenails that were painted a bright coral color.

As his gaze swept over her, he felt the slow spread of liquid yearning through his veins, an actual physical ache that was only exacerbated by the realization that he couldn't have her. Though he knew the attraction he felt wasn't entirely one-sided, there was no getting around the fact that he was supposed to be looking for a bride and Lara, as the children's nanny, was strictly off-limits.

Throughout the meal she made an effort to engage each of the children in conversation, helping them to share stories about the events of their day with him. But Rowan noticed that she didn't speak directly to him and she pushed more food around her plate than she actually ate, leading him to wonder if she was dissatisfied with the menu or if she was one of those women who rarely did more than nibble.

Christian, on the other hand, ate like a typical teenage boy. He'd already finished his first plate and was pouring gravy over another heaping mound of roast beef and potatoes. Lexi picked at her food without a lot of enthusiasm, while Damon had made a road through his mashed potatoes and was driving two peas along the track.

"Does the child not know how to use a fork?" he asked, not bothering to hide his exasperation.

Lara shot him a look of annoyance before turning to the boy. "You're supposed to eat your food, not play with it," she reminded him gently.

Damon picked up a piece of meat, popped it into his mouth, then went back to his race.

"And you're not s'posed to use your fingers," Lexi told him primly.

"Says who?" Damon demanded, glancing at Rowan out of the corner of his eye as if in challenge.

"Says Mommy."

His attention turned back to his sister. "Well, Mommy's not here."

Lexi's eyes filled with tears. "If she was, she'd tell you not to use your fingers."

"But she's not and you can't—"

"Damon." Lara interrupted his rant, her tone quiet but firm. "You shouldn't have to be reminded about appropriate behavior at the table."

The boy pouted but picked up his neglected fork and stabbed a carrot.

Lexi sniffled and wiped her nose with her sleeve.

Rowan bit his tongue. He'd hoped this "family" dinner would provide an opportunity to share a meal and some conversation with his brother's children, and he wasn't pleased by the children's bickering—or by the nanny's failure to take control of the situation.

Figuring his best chance for conversation was with his oldest nephew, he turned his attention in that direction. "I saw you were on the computer in the library earlier," he said to Christian.

The older boy nodded, his mouth full. He waited until he'd swallowed to respond further, reassuring Rowan that at least one of his brother's children had decent table manners. "Doing online research."

"What were you researching?"

"Causes of explosions on watercraft."

Lara's fork clattered against her plate. "Christian."

He shrugged. "I just want to understand what happened, why they di—"

"Stop right there." Her gaze was stormy as it locked on Christian's across the table.

"He asked." The boy shrugged again. "I just answered his question."

"'He' is your uncle," Lara reminded him. "And this isn't appropriate dinner conversation."

"Then what should we talk about?" Christian challenged. "What topics are suitable for fake family dinners?"

So much for thinking the kid had manners. Rowan reined in his own temper and responded coolly, "This meal is a chance to get to know each other better, and I expect you to make an effort to do that."

"Like you're making an effort?" The boy snorted. "The only reason you're even here now instead of living your own life in London is that Mom and Dad stuck you with guardianship."

"That's not true," Rowan said.

"Bull."

Damon goggled at his brother; Lexi started to cry again; and Lara just looked from Christian to Rowan, her pointed gaze telling him that he was going to have to work this out on his own. As if he had the slightest idea how to work out anything with a twelve-year-old boy who clearly resented everything about him.

"That kind of language isn't acceptable anywhere," he said in a low voice.

"You can't tell me what to do or say," Christian shot back. "You're not my father."

"No, I'm not," he agreed. "But you will speak to me with respect or you will leave this table."

Christian shoved his chair away from the table and stormed out of the room, past the server who hovered in the doorway with a silver pot in her hand.

Rowan held back a sigh as he beckoned to Maria, who poured coffee for both Lara and him, then exited the room quickly.

Lara added a splash of cream to her cup, then turned her attention to the two younger children.

"Are you finished eating?" she asked them.

Rowan frowned at the amount of food still left on their plates but said nothing as both Lexi and Damon nodded.

"Go wash up," she said. "Then you can go into the kitchen and ask Marcel if he has any more of that home-made ice cream."

Both faces brightened and they scampered off together.

He figured she wanted the children gone so they could discuss his verbal confrontation with Christian, but she remained silent, stirring her coffee.

She might be prepared to ignore the boy's behavior, but Rowan was not. "He's going to have to learn to control his impulses."

Lara lifted her cup, sipped.

"His outburst was inappropriate and his language was vulgar," he continued.

"You should focus on the content rather than the delivery," she finally said. "If you did, you'd realize that what he said was a true expression of his feelings."

"It was inappropriate," he said again.

"But not inaccurate."

He frowned at that. "What do you mean?"

"I mean that he was right. I might not go so far as to say this dinner plan was fake, but it was superficial, and until you—and I mean all of you—make an honest effort to get to know one another, you can't expect anything else."

"Doesn't this—" he gestured around the table "—prove that I'm making an effort?"

She opened her mouth as if to speak, then closed it again without uttering a word.

"Say it."

"You don't want to hear it," she warned.

"Probably not," he agreed. "But that's never stopped you before."

"Okay. I don't think this—" she gestured as he had done "—proves anything. And those kids are smart enough to know that you're just going through the motions so that you can tell yourself you tried."

"You have a better idea?" he challenged.

"You have to acknowledge your feelings and resentments."

"I have no resentments."

"And stop lying to yourself," she added.

"Who or what am I supposed to resent?"

"Julian and Catherine for dying, the laws of succession for putting you in charge, the children for making you aware of your shortcomings. Actually, the whole situation."

He laughed. "You're not serious?"

"Emotions aren't logical or reasonable," she said patiently. "And you're never going to connect with those children and really become a family if you don't deal with the negative feelings."

"And what makes you an expert on family dynamics?"

"I'm not claiming to be an expert, but I do believe that honesty and communication are the keys to making any relationship work. And one shared meal isn't going to cut it."

"Well, this is new territory for me," he admitted. "And I'm doing the best that I can."

"Your best has to be better," she said bluntly.

Before he could respond, Lexi and Damon came back into the dining room.

"I thought you might want some dessert, too." Lexi placed one of the bowls she'd balanced on her hands in front of Rowan, then gave the other one to Lara.

He was surprised—and touched—by the gesture, and he figured his effort couldn't have been too bad if his niece was bringing him ice cream. "Thank you, Alexandria."

"That was very thoughtful," Lara said. Then, as Damon crawled into her lap, she asked the boy, "Are you sleepy?"

He nodded and yawned as he settled his head against her shoulder.

"Then it's bath time for you," she said, rising from her

chair with the little boy in her arms. "We need to wash all that sticky ice cream off before you fall asleep."

"Aren't you gonna eat your dessert?" Lexi asked.

"Maybe later. I have to get your brother ready for bed before he falls asleep standing up."

"But it'll melt."

"Not if you take it back to the kitchen and ask Marcel to put it in the freezer."

"Or I could eat it," the little girl suggested hopefully.

"You've already had dessert," Lara reminded her.

"Please?" she turned beseeching eyes on him, and he melted far more quickly than the ice cream would.

"No," Lara said, at the same time he answered, "Sure."

Alexandria's brow furrowed.

"Lexi knows that she's not supposed to ask for ice cream more than once a day," she explained to him.

"But she didn't ask the first time," he couldn't resist saying. "You offered it."

Her only response was to narrow her gaze as she shifted Damon in her arms.

"Does that mean I get the ice cream?" Lexi asked.

"Sure," Rowan said again, enjoying the wide smile she flashed at him before digging into the treat.

"I'm taking Damon upstairs," Lara said. "Come on up when you're finished, Lexi, and I'll get your bath ready."

"'Kay," the little girl answered around a mouthful of dessert.

Rowan watched the sway of Lara's hips as she walked out of the dining room, baffled that he could want a woman even though he always seemed to be at odds with her. Or maybe he deliberately provoked her to ensure they remained at odds, knowing it was the only sure way to keep her at a distance and keep his hands off her.

* * *

Lara closed the book she wasn't reading and lifted her head to look out the window.

There was a light breeze coming off the water, and though she couldn't see anything but stars in the darkness, she could hear the gurgle of the fountains, the chirp of the crickets, and smell the flowers in the garden below.

Her gaze drifted across the courtyard, as if drawn to the light that flicked on, illuminating a corner window on the second floor of the north tower. Rowan's office.

The light stayed on long into the night most evenings when he was home, and she wasn't surprised to find that it was on now, that he was working late again.

His new role as prince regent was a huge responsibility and, unlike Julian, Rowan didn't have a partner who could assume some of the duties and lessen his burden. She'd worried that he was pushing himself too hard, that he'd been too preoccupied with his new responsibilities to let himself grieve for the loss of his brother and sister-in-law. When he'd fired her, she'd revised her assessment, certain that a man who had no heart couldn't experience grief.

In either case, it wasn't her problem.

But when he'd shown up at Luke's house and said he needed her, she knew she wouldn't be able to refuse.

All her life, she'd been made to feel that nothing she did was quite good enough, that *she* wasn't good enough. Her mom had often suggested that if only Lara had been prettier or smarter or better behaved, her dad might have wanted to stick around. Instead she'd grown up without a father and with a mother who resented her more and more with each year that passed. And then she'd lost her mother, too.

She'd wanted nothing more than to be wanted. Being needed was, she figured, the next best thing.

She knew that the prince regent didn't want her any more than anyone else ever had, but he needed her.

Even if he didn't know how much.

She wondered if she'd been a little harsh earlier, then decided not. Her own personal feelings about the man aside, it was important for the children to know their uncle, and vice versa. And if he was ever going to have a good relationship with Christian, Lexi and Damon, he had to start building that relationship now.

With a determination only slighter greater than her trepidation, she wound her way through the maze of the palace from her rooms to Rowan's office.

She noted that the desk outside his door was unmanned and guessed Rowan had dismissed his secretary earlier because he hadn't intended to return to work that night. She wondered now if he'd come back because there were pressing matters of state to attend to or because he was seeking refuge from his thoughts in paperwork.

The door was ajar, and she could hear soft music emanating from within. Julian had always insisted on quiet when he was working, but Rowan seemed to prefer having music in the background. She stepped closer, her hand raised to knock. Through the opening she could see him behind his desk, looking at the picture perched on the corner. The naked anguish visible on his handsome face stunned her.

Her hand fell to her side.

Here was the emotion she'd thought he was incapable of feeling—and more. Grief and anger and sorrow and frustration—so clear and raw and powerful they seemed to reach out and squeeze her heart. She didn't know what precisely had cracked the seemingly impenetrable facade, only that something had and he was hurting.

Indecision warred within her. She wanted to flee, to leave him to confront his pain and his demons alone. And she wanted to go to him, to wrap her arms around him and do anything she could to ease his heartache. But she knew he wouldn't thank her for witnessing this uncharacteristic display. He probably wouldn't even forgive her.

In the end she simply raised her hand again and knocked.

"Enter."

She pushed the door open a little wider and stepped into his office. Sure enough, the shadows she'd glimpsed in his eyes were already masked, the tension in his jaw relaxed.

"Yes, Miss Brennan?"

"I'm sorry for interrupting," she said, "but I wanted to apologize."

"For neglecting to tell me that Alexandria is lactose intolerant?" he guessed.

She winced. "I didn't expect that she'd actually throw up on you."

"Well, you made your point," he told her.

"What point was that?"

"That I don't have a clue when it comes to what the children need."

"And now you're going to use that as an excuse to take another step back from them," she guessed.

He shook his head. "They don't need me."

"If you believe that, then you really don't have a clue."

"Were you at the same dinner table I was?"

"Yes, and I saw three children who recently lost both of their parents seeking confirmation that they matter to someone. The rest of the family is unavailable to them—Eric is at sea more than he's home, Marcus is at law school in America, and their grandparents went back to Ireland after the funeral. You're the only one they have here and in the past three weeks you've only managed to find the time to share one meal with them."

"In case it's escaped your notice," he said, "I've been busy trying to run this country."

"I know there are a lot of demands on your time, but right now the children need you more than all of the politicians and lobby groups and charities and committees in Tesoro del Mar combined.

"They need *you*," she said again, more softly this time. "Maybe as much as you need them."

He frowned at that but didn't debate the point. "At least there's *one* thing I can feel confident that I've done right with respect to the children."

"What's that?"

"I convinced you to come back."

She flushed in response to the unexpected compliment but wasn't willing to let him abdicate responsibility so easily. "I'm their nanny. You're their family."

He was quiet for a minute, then nodded. "I'll try to make a better effort."

She wanted to see him back up his words with action but decided to give him the benefit of the doubt.

At least for now.

Chapter Five

The last thing Rowan wanted was another confrontation with an obviously angry and grieving child. But after his conversation with Lara, he knew he couldn't leave things the way they were with Christian.

He found the boy in the library, on the computer again, and wondered why Julian hadn't had one set up in his son's bedroom. He was going to suggest exactly that, thinking it might serve as a peace offering to break down some of the barriers between them. Then he remembered his recent resolution not to make any decisions about the children without consulting the nanny first and stifled the impulse.

"What are you doing?" he asked instead, noting the rapid movement of his nephew's fingers over the keyboard.

"Chatting."

Rowan knew that if he waited for the boy to expand on

his explanation, he'd wait a long time. "Could you take a break, please? I'd like to talk to you."

"I can do two things at once."

He felt his teeth grind together, but recognized that he'd made a mistake in asking a question rather than issuing a command. "I'm sure you can, but right now, we're going to focus on one. You're going to log off the computer and talk to me."

The boy's brows slammed together as he hit a few more keys, then he shoved the keyboard away and turned to his uncle with a mutinous expression. "I'm logged off."

"Thank you."

"Did you come to make me apologize for the things I said at dinner?"

"Do you feel an apology is warranted?"

He rolled his shoulders. "Maybe."

Rowan only lifted a brow.

"Fine—I'm sorry I was disrespectful," he said in a tone that was anything but respectful. "Are we done now?"

"Not even close. The things you said at dinner are only the beginning."

Christian's eyes narrowed. "Lara put you up to this, didn't she?"

"Why would you think that?"

"Because you've never shown any interest in any of us before."

His nephew didn't sound hurt or angry. He was simply stating what he believed. Maybe that was why the guilt struck so deep.

"I'm sorry that's how you perceived the situation," Rowan said, then immediately shook his head. "No, I'm sorry that's the way it's been."

Christian eyed him warily. "You're not going to tell me I'm wrong?"

"It's not that I don't care about all of you, but I realize I haven't shown much of an interest, and for that I'm sorry."

The kid shrugged again. "It's not your fault. My mom and dad should have made sure you wanted us before making you our guardian."

"We did talk about it," Rowan admitted. "A long time ago."

"You did?"

"I had no objections to being named as your guardian, but the truth is, I never really thought about what it meant. Your parents were both young and healthy. It never occurred to me that something like this might happen."

"Something like what?"

Rowan unlocked a drawer in his desk and pulled out a thick folder emblazoned with the crest of the Royal Navy. "A blast originating in the engine room of the *Lysithea*— the combined result of a gas-line leak and a spark generated by the electrical engine switch."

Christian stared at the folder in his uncle's hand. "You're going to let me read the report?"

Though there had been rumblings that it was a conflict of interest for Eric to be involved in the investigation of the explosion that killed his brother and sister-in-law, he'd refused to be shut out. And he'd made sure that Rowan and Marcus each got copies, not just of the official findings, but of all the documentation that had gone into the making of that final report. The brothers had needed that information to understand and accept the deaths, and Rowan realized now that his nephew did, too.

"You have a right to know," he said.

"But understanding how it happened won't change anything, will it?" Christian asked, showing insight beyond his years.

"It won't bring them back," he agreed.

The boy dropped his gaze to the top of the desk. "It's so hard to believe they're gone. There are times when I still expect Dad to walk though the door, when I wait for Mom to poke her head in my room and ask if I want to go riding."

"I miss them, too," Rowan admitted.

Silence stretched between them for a long moment, but it was easier now. Not exactly comfortable, but not filled with tension and animosity, either.

"I really am sorry about the things I said at dinner," Christian finally said, sounding sincere this time.

"I appreciate your apology." Rowan moved across the room, satisfied with the progress they'd made and not wanting to push the boy for anything more.

But he hesitated at the door, and when he turned back, he saw Christian was watching him. "I like to ride," he said. "Usually early mornings are the only chance I get, but I don't mind company."

The boy's tentative smile squeezed his heart. "Maybe I'll see you at the stables one morning."

"Maybe."

When Lara came to Tesoro del Mar, she knew nothing about horses. The first time she went down to the stables, it was Marcus who had taken her there. He'd been shocked to realize that she didn't know how to ride and insisted that she learn, and he'd made it his personal mission to teach her.

Lara had enjoyed their lessons—and Marcus's shameless flirting. Maybe it was because he was close to her own age, or maybe it was that he clearly didn't worry about the pomp and protocol that went along with being a royal, but she was more comfortable with him than with any of his brothers and soon they became good friends. She also learned how to ride.

Marcus had applauded her as an eager and gifted student; she was certain her success was more the result of his skill as a teacher. Because, as much as the youngest Santiago brother might enjoy his reputation as a man who had no sense of purpose or direction except if it took him toward the nearest pub or a willing woman, Lara quickly learned that there was a lot more to the playboy prince than he wanted people to know. And she'd realized that he had a passion for and commitment to the horses that exceeded his interest in or affection for anything or anyone else.

She'd been given leave to ride whenever she wished, and generally chose Regal Lady as her mount when she did so. The red roan mare was as gentle as she was strong, and Lara loved the feel of racing over the fields on her back, the mare's hooves pounding the ground, the wind whipping through her hair.

She pushed open the stable doors and stepped inside, smiling as she inhaled the familiar earthy scents of hay and horses. She made her way down the cobblestone corridor that divided the rows of stalls, pausing now and again to stroke a long nose that poked over a gate to investigate the sound of her approaching footsteps. She stopped in front of Regal Lady's stall and couldn't hold back her sigh of disappointment when she found it empty.

"Eddie took Lady out," a gruff voice said from behind her.

"Oh." She turned to Frank, the stable manager, and lifted a shoulder. "I just thought I'd peek in and see if she needed some exercise."

"She'll be sorry she missed you," he said so solemnly she couldn't help but smile.

"Maybe I'll try to get down here again later in the week."

"Maybe you could try another mount today."

Lara hesitated.

"Royal Folly could use a good run," Frank told her.

As if on cue, the chestnut stallion in the neighboring stall pawed the ground and snorted out an impatient breath. While Lara had always admired the animal's powerful build and proud carriage, she'd also been more than a little intimidated by the creature. Not to mention the fact that Folly had been Princess Catherine's horse.

She wanted to refuse, not certain she had the skill or strength to control him, but before she could say anything, the stallion bumped his head against her shoulder. She turned and found herself staring into soulful dark eyes. Instinctively she brushed her hand down his nose, rubbing gently. "You miss her, too, don't you?" she murmured softly.

The stallion tossed his head, in agreement or impatience, she wasn't sure, but in that moment her decision was made.

"They all do," Frank said, his gruff tone indicating that it wasn't just the horses that were missing the princess's presence down at the stables. "But Folly probably more than most."

"You think I can handle him, Frank?"

His nod was abrupt. "Prince Marcus taught you to ride, didn't he?"

"He did," she agreed.

"Then I have no doubts."

"Okay, then," she said to Folly, rubbing her hand down his muzzle again. "Looks like you and I have a date."

Though she was more than capable of tacking her own mount, she let Frank help her with the task. He liked to remind her that it was his job to oversee everything that had anything to do with the horses and that it was a job he'd been doing for more than forty years now. He also liked to talk while he worked, so almost half an hour passed before Lara was in the saddle and riding away from the stables.

She could feel Folly's excitement in the quivering flank clamped between her thighs as she fought to maintain control, at least until they'd reached more open ground. Then she nudged him with her heels, and they flew across the fields.

Rowan heard the pounding of hooves, was aware of the horse and rider drawing nearer, but didn't move out of the shadows. He hoped that if he stayed hidden, they would race right past. He'd come out here to be alone, to steal some much needed solitude and breathing space.

No one but Frank knew he was here, and when the pounding slowed, he silently cursed the end of this peaceful interlude. He wasn't nearly ready to return to the palace and the obligations that awaited him there, but he knew if the old groom had tracked him down, it was because he was needed somewhere.

The rider steered the stallion toward the creek.

Definitely not Frank.

Lara.

It wasn't the shiny copper hair that gave her identity away, but the sharp punch of lust that hit low in his belly when his gaze landed on her. That familiar and frustrating reaction was unmistakable. Undeniable.

He'd had a similar instinctive response to only one other

woman—Margot Olivier. He knew that Lara wasn't Margot, just as he knew that he wasn't the same man he'd been when he fell in love with the stunning coed more than a dozen years before. He'd grown up and he'd changed, in no small part because of the experience with his conniving girlfriend. And he'd vowed that he would never open up his heart so completely again—and he'd never been tempted to do so.

Until Lara.

She haunted his thoughts when he was awake, his dreams when he was sleeping, and now even this stolen moment of solitude was no longer his own.

As he watched her descend from the top of the hill, he saw that she sat a horse well, obviously confident and comfortable in the saddle. The jeans she wore were faded and slim fitting, hugging narrow hips and a waist that he could probably span with his hands. Her blouse was sleeveless, showing long toned arms and just a hint of cleavage where the top few buttons were undone.

She slid off the back of the horse, rubbed her hand over his cheek and murmured something that he couldn't hear. As she turned to lead him down to the creek to drink, Rowan saw the tears on her own cheeks.

Before he could remind himself of the thousand reasons it was a bad idea, he moved out of the shadows and went to her.

She jolted when he touched her arm. "Your Highness! I didn't realize anyone was here."

"Obviously." Her lashes were wet and spiky, her emerald eyes shimmering. Her nose was red, her cheeks were streaked with tears, and she was still so beautiful. He pulled a handkerchief from his pocket and offered it to her.

"Thank you." She accepted the neatly pressed square of

linen, wiped her cheeks. "I don't want to intrude. As soon as Folly's finished drinking, we'll go."

"Don't." He hadn't thought he wanted company or that he would want hers in particular, but now that she was here, he realized he wanted her there.

"You wanted privacy," she guessed.

He sat back down, hoping to put her at ease. "That's what I thought, but now I realize I just wanted to get away for a while."

When she still looked uncertain, he added, "Stay. Please."

She lowered herself to the ground—a couple of feet away from him. He wasn't sure if he should be insulted or amused by her obvious attempt to keep him at a distance.

"How is it that you have free time in the middle of the day?" she asked him.

"I rescheduled a meeting with the minister of finance, then had Lionel cancel my lunch with the VP of the Arts Council."

"Ah, so you're playing hooky."

"I prefer to think of it as creative scheduling."

She smiled at him, and he felt something curl deep inside.

"How did you find this place?" he asked her.

"Princess Catherine and I used to bring the kids here for picnics. Prince Julian, too, sometimes, if he could manage some creative scheduling."

"Did you know that Julian proposed to Catherine out here—right under this tree, in fact?"

"No, I didn't." She leaned back on her elbows, her face tilted up to the sun. As she shifted, so did his attention—to the open neck of her shirt, the creamy vee of skin that was visible where the material parted. "But she did tell me that the first time he ever kissed her was out here."

"He probably would have tried to do more than kiss her if Eric hadn't fallen out of the tree almost right on top of them."

"Eric was spying on them?"

"Marcus and I were spying on them," he admitted. "Eric came with us because he could climb high enough in the tree to see the boats out at sea. Even as a kid he wanted nothing more than to be on the water."

"I bet Julian wasn't too pleased with any of you that day."

"He was furious," Rowan admitted.

She smiled again, and his gaze was drawn to her mouth, lingered there. Her lips were the palest pink, like the inside of a shell, and exquisitely shaped. He didn't know that he'd ever been so fascinated by a woman's mouth before, or so tempted.

He wondered what she would do if he leaned over now and touched his mouth to hers. Would she kiss him back? Or push him away? Would she taste cool, like the water flowing in the stream? Or hot, like the blood churning in his veins?

He lifted his eyes and met hers.

For a long moment neither of them said anything. There was no sound but the rustle of the leaves in the breeze. No one around but the two of them.

He was suddenly aware of how far away they were from the palace, from the rules and responsibilities that governed there, from the pressure that was being exerted on him to find a suitable bride. Here he could almost believe he wasn't a prince and she wasn't a nanny. They were just a man and a woman, with no barriers between them.

"It's hard to accept that they're gone, isn't it?" she said softly.

The question jerked him out of his fantasy.

"I was thinking about them," she continued. "On my way here. Remembering the times we'd been here together."

"That's why you were crying."

She nodded, but said nothing else, only reached out briefly to touch his arm. An offer of comfort, friendship.

As he sat and talked with her in the afternoon sun, he found himself accepting her offer, and grateful for it. Except for one problem: he didn't want her comfort or friendship. He wanted Lara.

Chapter Six

Over the next few weeks, Lara found herself spending more time with the prince regent and his niece and nephews. She was pleased to find that there was more to Rowan than the solemn prince that he let the rest of the world see, and she was thrilled to watch as the children gradually warmed toward their uncle.

But it was difficult for her, because the more she saw him with the children, the more she saw the warm and compassionate side of him and the more attracted she was to the man. She wished she could disregard her feelings as an irrational hormonal attraction, but with every day that passed, her feelings were growing and deepening.

The man Tanis liked to refer to as His Royal Arrogance was actually more down-to-earth than she would have expected. She'd seen him smile, heard him laugh, and while the cynical part of her wanted to believe that he was making an effort to lighten up so the children would like him, she knew it wasn't true.

And the more she got to know him, the more she wanted to know. Beyond the attraction she'd felt from the very beginning, she found herself genuinely liking him—and that was a complication she hadn't anticipated.

The children were a little more ambivalent in their feelings—or so she'd thought until they approached her with their idea.

"A birthday party?" Lara echoed dubiously.

"A surprise party," Lexi said.

Damon clapped his hands together. "Party! Party!"

She hesitated and glanced at Christian. He was the only one who had yet to speak and, as usual, she couldn't begin to guess what he was thinking.

"I'm not sure that's a good idea," she said. "He might already have plans."

"Christian checked with Henri to make sure it was okay," Lexi told her.

Her older brother confirmed this information with a solemn nod. "His calendar is open between six and eight tonight."

Lara still had her doubts, but the children were clearly united in their desire to throw a party for their uncle and she didn't want to disappoint them. "Well, then, I guess we have a celebration to plan."

"He's coming! He's coming!" Damon announced, racing back into the prince's office that had been lavishly decorated with colorful streamers and bouquets of helium-filled balloons.

Lara had given up trying to stop him from dipping his fingers into the thick chocolate icing of the cake they'd made. To distance him from the temptation, she'd assigned him the task of watching for his uncle.

"Is he really this time?" Christian asked, clearly losing patience with the little brother who had made the same announcement three times already, then dissolved into a fit of giggles while they all waited silently in the darkness.

"Really, really, for true," Damon insisted.

With a last look around the room to ensure that everything was in its place, Lara hit the switch to kill the lights. Damon snuggled close to her when it went dark, his little body fairly vibrating with excitement.

Lexi stood closest to the door, with handfuls of glittery confetti she planned to toss at her uncle when he entered the room. Lara had tried to talk her out of that one, but the little girl would not be dissuaded.

She felt her stomach knot as she tried to anticipate Rowan's reaction to the surprise. He might be annoyed rather than pleased, but at least he was here. One of her biggest worries had been that the prince might not come home after his meeting ended because he'd had a more personal celebration planned for his birthday. She'd been reassured when Henri offered to help with the party, certain he would have discouraged the children if he believed the party was a mistake. Or maybe he *had* tried to discourage them and had run into the same wall of determination that had blocked Lara's protests.

In any event, it was too late to back out now.

She heard the murmur of voices in the hall, drawing nearer, and felt the knots in her stomach tighten.

"If you could just take a look at the papers now, then we can discuss them at greater length in the morning."

"Can't they wait until the morning?" Rowan asked wearily. "I'm supposed to be meeting—"

"I'm aware of your schedule," Henri told him.

It occurred to Lara that Henri's interruption was intended to prevent the prince from revealing details about the meeting to her and the children. Because the meeting was about a sensitive political matter? she wondered. Or because he was meeting a woman?

"So much for the ruler's birthday being a national holiday," Rowan muttered.

"Only for everyone else," Henri told him.

Finally the door was pushed open and the lights went on.

"Surprise!" The children yelled in unison, though Lexi and Damon with significantly more enthusiasm and volume than their older brother.

Then Lexi remembered the confetti and tossed it high in the air, showering tiny silver-colored stars all over her uncle and everything else in the vicinity.

Rowan's lips curved slowly as his gaze moved around the room, noting the colorful decorations, the small stack of presents and the slightly lopsided chocolate cake on the silver tray in the center of his desk.

"It looks like someone's having a party," he said.

Lexi beamed. "It's a birthday party for you."

"A surprise party," Damon piped up.

"It certainly is that." Rowan glanced at Henri, hovering in the doorway and smiling. "I assume those papers you mentioned were merely a ruse."

"Yes, Your Highness."

"Then I have no other business tonight?"

"Just that one meeting."

"Which you can cancel, Henri."

"Sir?" His friend and advisor was clearly taken aback by this instruction.

"I'd like to spend what is left of my birthday with my family."

"Of course." Henri bowed and ducked back out of the office.

Rowan stepped farther into the room, his eyes on the cake. "How many candles are on there?"

"Thirty-five," Damon told him. "I counted 'em to be sure, 'cause Lara said that's how really old you are."

"I told him that's how old you really are," she quickly corrected, conscious of the heat that filled her cheeks. "Not that you're really old."

But Rowan didn't seem offended, his eyes sparkling with humor when they turned to her. "I imagine thirty-five seems really old to a four-year-old."

"And an eight-year-old," Lexi agreed, throwing in her lot with her brother.

"Did you know you can be thrown into the dungeon for insulting a member of the royal family?" Rowan asked her.

"I am a member of the royal family," she reminded him in a tone that left no doubt about the blue in her blood. "And the dungeons were closed before the end of the last century. I learned that at school. And that means no one can be thrown into the dungeon anymore."

"What's a dungeon?" Damon wanted to know.

Rowan squatted beside the boy and lowered his voice to an ominous whisper. "A cold, dark room deep beneath the castle where naughty little boys and girls are kept shackled and fed only bread and water."

Damon's eyes widened and he took a step back before asking, "What's shackled?"

"Tied up in chains," Lexi told him. "And no one's going to be shackled or put in the dungeon."

"Did they tell you who closed the dungeon?" Rowan asked his niece.

She shook her head.

"It was my grandfather, His Royal Highness Prince Emmanuel of Tesoro del Mar, because only the ruler has the authority to make that kind of decision. And if he could close them—" he narrowed his gaze menacingly "—I can open them up again just for you."

The little girl only lifted her chin. "But you won't," she said confidently. "Because you're a good ruler and a good uncle."

The furrow in Rowan's brow smoothed and his gaze softened.

Lara felt her throat tighten as he reached out to touch his niece. He was a man who made decisions without hesitation, who carried himself with arrogant confidence, who never faltered. But when he stroked his hand over Lexi's hair, she saw not just the uncertainty in the gesture, but the vulnerability in his heart, and felt her own soften.

"I don't know that I've always been a good uncle," he said. "But I'm trying now."

Lexi smiled at him, a child's smile full of warmth and affection. "You're doing okay."

"Does that mean I get a slice of that cake?"

"After the games," Damon said.

"Games?" Rowan asked.

"They're set up in the media room," Lexi said, tugging on his hand. "Come on."

The games were more for the benefit of the children, but Lara was impressed by Rowan's willingness to play along. He took a turn tossing bean bags into a can, participated in musical chairs, allowed himself to be blindfolded and spun around for Pin the Tail on the Donkey, and swung a plastic bat at the dinosaur piñata, finally breaking it open and spilling candy all over the floor for the children to scoop up.

When the games were done, they returned to Rowan's office so that he could open his presents.

Damon offered his first—a heavy oblong-shaped package that was covered with as much tape as it was paper. Rowan took his time admiring the careful printing of his youngest nephew's name on the card before tearing the paper off his gift.

"It's a pet rock," Damon told his uncle. "Lara says you can use it as a paperweight."

"A pet, huh?" Rowan looked the painted stone over carefully. "Does it eat much?"

Damon giggled. "It doesn't eat anything."

The prince regent looked skeptical. "Are you sure about that? Because I don't want to have to share my birthday cake with it."

"I'm sure," the little boy told him.

"Do this one next," Lexi said, handing him a larger and flatter package that was more neatly wrapped. "It's from Christian."

Rowan opened the card—this one store-bought rather than homemade—and scrawled simply with Christian's signature. But though the card might have been impersonal, the gift was not.

Christian had shown it to her before he'd wrapped it, wanting to know if she thought it was an appropriate present for his uncle. Lara had been sure Rowan would love it, and she could tell by the surprised pleasure in his eyes that she'd been right.

It was a framed picture of Rowan and his brothers with their father, all of them on horseback, the sky behind them washed in streaks of yellow and orange and crimson by the setting sun.

"I haven't seen this in years," Rowan murmured.

"I was looking through some old photo albums for pictures of my dad, and I found it." Christian dropped his gaze and shrugged, clearly more than a little self-conscious. "I thought you might like it."

The prince swallowed as he stared at the photo in the thick cherrywood frame. "I do. I like it a lot."

"I have something for you, too," Lexi said, taking the last present to him.

Rowan propped Christian's picture on his desk beside Damon's rock before accepting Lexi's gift.

Hers was another picture, this one painted by the little girl and showing remarkable talent for an eight-year-old child. "It's a picture of you and me and Christian and Damon," she told him, pointing to each in turn. "'Cause we're like a family now."

"We *are* a family," he agreed, then kissed the top of her head. "And it's beautiful. Thank you."

"Now can we have cake?" Damon asked Lara, his tone suggesting that he'd been waiting forever.

She took a box of matches out of her pocket and struck one.

"Wait," Christian said, halting her before she could touch the flame to the wick of the first candle.

He hadn't said very much throughout the proceedings, but now he had everyone's attention. He ducked outside the office and came back a minute later with something held behind his back and a rare smile on his face.

"Okay." He set a fire extinguisher on the desk beside the cake, his smile growing wider. "Now we're ready."

As Lara lit the candles, she realized it was the first joke

Christian had made in weeks, and she let herself believe it was a sign that the pain of Julian's and Catherine's deaths was starting to fade. She set the cake in front of Rowan and wished the same was true for him, too.

Rowan wasn't usually one for late-night forays into the kitchen—if he wanted a snack or a drink at any time, he only had to summon one of the servants and the object of his desire would be promptly delivered to him. Just one of the fringe benefits of being a prince, and one that he appreciated but didn't take advantage of. If it was after midnight—as it was now—he always tried to fend for himself, which was why he was on his way to the kitchen, lured by the temptation of leftover chocolate cake.

Making his way through the maze of corridors, he found himself thinking about the events of the afternoon. Considering the effort the children had gone to in planning and executing the party—even enlisting Henri's help to ensure he attended—he figured they were warming up to him.

He was glad about that, and grateful to Lara for helping them to adjust to the numerous changes of late. Yes, gratitude was an emotion he could acknowledge and accept, though certainly not the only one she stirred in him.

He shook his head and tried to force all thoughts of her from his mind by mentally sorting through the highlights of his day. He thought fleetingly of the "meeting" he'd asked Henri to cancel, which had actually been plans for a private and very personal birthday celebration with Vivian Winters. He'd known Viv for years, and though they'd been occasional lovers during that time, neither of them had expectations for anything more. Still, he owed her a phone call and an explanation.

He decided he'd take his cake back to his apartment and

call Viv from there. It occurred to him that he might be able to entice her into joining him for dessert, but he discarded the thought almost immediately. Now that he'd celebrated his thirty-fifth birthday, he was suddenly aware the clock was ticking.

He had only six months to marry, and though he was fond of Vivian, he couldn't imagine her as his bride. The problem was, he couldn't imagine any woman he knew as his bride, and he couldn't help but resent the circumstances that were demanding he choose one.

Then he stepped into the kitchen and forgot about his marriage deadline and everyone and everything else except the woman standing at the counter. She'd changed out of the long flowing skirt and gauzy blouse she'd been wearing earlier and into a pair of dark yoga pants that sat low on her hips and a skimpy tank top that molded to her breasts. She looked casual, comfortable and far too enticing for his peace of mind.

He was suddenly conscious of the fact that, though the tie had been loosened and the jacket discarded, he was still wearing the suit he'd put on that morning. The formality of his own attire seemed to be yet another reminder of the numerous differences between them, the many reasons he shouldn't feel the way he did about her. He should go— forget about the cake and forget about Lara—but he found himself moving toward her rather than away.

"Stealing the royal birthday cake?" he queried.

She whirled around. "Only a small slice," she said, her cheeks flushing prettily. "We barely made a dent in it earlier."

"Then you might as well make it a big slice—actually, two big slices."

"I can do that," she agreed, reaching into the cupboard for another plate.

"What are you doing up so late?" he wondered. "Did Damon have another nightmare?"

She shook her head. "No, thank goodness. He's slept through a few nights now—I couldn't say how many for sure, because I don't want to jinx it by counting."

"Are you superstitious, Miss Brennan?"

"Not really, but I don't believe in tempting fate, either." She pulled open a drawer and took out two forks. She clearly knew her way around the kitchen—far more than he did.

"Glasses?" he asked her.

She gestured to an overhead cupboard.

He stepped closer, close enough to catch a whiff of the scent she wore—something light and subtle but unmistakably feminine and undeniably arousing.

She shifted to drop the cake server into the sink, and as she did, the curve of her buttocks brushed against the front of his trousers.

Mi Dios.

His fingers tightened on the handle of the cupboard.

"I beg your pardon, Your Highness." The words were spoken softly, huskily.

"No harm done," he told her, though he wasn't entirely sure it was true.

Over the past few weeks, he'd been so careful to keep a safe distance between them. But the distance hadn't done anything to lessen his desire for her, as the bolt of lust that shot through him in response to that brief and incidental contact proved.

He waited until she'd stepped away, then took two glasses from the cupboard and filled them with milk.

"You didn't say why you were still up," he noted.

She carried the plates to the table. He followed with

their drinks. "I was finishing up a research paper on the benefits of learning through play."

"A research paper?" He sat across from her at the butcher-block table in the kitchen while they both indulged their midnight cravings. But while the cake satisfied his physical hunger, being with Lara made him all too aware of other desires that remained unfulfilled.

She poked at her cake. "I'm working toward my teaching certificate."

"I didn't realize you were attending the university."

"Only part-time," she said quickly. "I'm always here when the children need my supervision."

"I was commenting, not criticizing," he told her.

"I'm sorry, Your Highness. I have a tendency to be defensive."

"And we have a tendency to always talk about the children," he noted. "I know almost nothing about your interests or ambitions, except that you apparently want to be a teacher."

"I love my job here," she assured him. "But the children won't need me forever, and I thought I should have a plan for the future."

"That sounds reasonable. And you clearly have a talent for working with children."

"Thank you," she murmured, as her cheeks flushed again.

He swallowed another mouthful of chocolate and tried not to think about the fact that she couldn't possibly be wearing a bra beneath that skimpy little top.

"This is great cake," he said, in an inane attempt to keep up their conversation, to keep her talking so she would stay there with him just a little bit longer.

"Marcel gave us the recipe and permission to invade his

kitchen," she told him. "If it had been up to me, I would have bought something from the bakery in town."

"Not much of a chef?"

"I can handle the basics," she said. "Enough so that I wouldn't starve if I had to fend for myself, but not much more than that."

"You'd never know it from the taste of this," he told her, lifting the fork to his mouth again.

"Lexi really did most of it. I just supervised—and retrieved the eggshells from the batter."

"Thank you for that."

She smiled and licked a smudge of icing off her thumb, drawing his attention to the moist pink tip of her tongue and conjuring up all kinds of wildly erotic and completely inappropriate images in his mind.

"I want to thank you," she said, "for being such a good sport about the birthday party. I wasn't sure how you'd react, but you know Lexi—when she gets an idea in her head, there's no telling her no."

He dragged his attention away from his illicit fantasies and back to their conversation. "I'm starting to know her," he agreed. "But right now, I'm curious about you."

"Why?" she asked warily, no doubt aware that he could find out anything he wanted to about her background with a few inquiries of his staff. And he'd been tempted to do just that, believing that the answers to his questions would help eradicate his inexplicable fascination with her. But he hadn't, not because he felt uncomfortable with the idea of going behind her back for information but because he wanted her to tell him.

"Where you grew up, for starters," he said. "I know my brother and sister-in-law met you in Ireland, but you don't have Catherine's Irish accent."

"My mom was Irish," she said. "But I was born in America. Colorado, actually."

He imagined rocky mountains and rugged cowboys and a country that was more than a world away from his own. "How did you end up back in Ireland?"

"My mother died, and I had no other family in America."

"What about your father?"

She dropped her gaze. "I never knew him."

He guessed that her father had passed away when she was very young, and he couldn't help but regret that she had no memories of him—as he feared would be the case for Damon. As much as Rowan hated knowing that his young nephew continued to be haunted by bad dreams, he suspected that the end of those nightmares would only come with the acceptance that his parents were gone, and that his memories would fade along with his dreams.

"How old were you when you lost your mother?"

"Fifteen." She mashed the crumbs on her plate with the back of her fork.

"Not much older than Christian is now," he noted.

She nodded. "I'd hoped that experiencing a similar kind of loss might help me to reach through his grief, but so far I haven't been able to do so. He's completely focused on his studies, as if nothing else matters. I don't even know if he's really let himself grieve."

He noted that she was much more comfortable talking about his nephew than she was about herself, and while he still had a lot more questions about Lara, she had succeeded in diverting his attention—at least for now.

"Julian always marveled at how intensely focused Christian was," Rowan told her.

"I've known him since he was Damon's age, and I used

to feel as if I did know him. Now I can't even guess what he's thinking or feeling. It's as if he's forgotten how to be a child, and I don't know how to help him."

"I'll try to talk to him."

She was visibly surprised by his offer, so much so that he didn't know whether to be amused or insulted.

"I didn't mean to put the onus on you," she said. "The children are my responsibility—"

"And Christian is my nephew."

"I realize that, of course. It's just that…" She gave a slight shake of her head. "Thank you. It could be that I'm not the right person for him to confide in, that he needs to talk to another man."

"Then you acknowledge that I am a man?"

Her fork clattered against her plate. "I beg your pardon?"

He couldn't help but smile as he reached up to smooth the furrow between her brows. His smile widened as her breath caught and every muscle in her body stilled.

"I've noticed that you refer to Marcus, Julian and Catherine by name, but you always call me 'Your Highness.' I wasn't sure if you saw past the title to realize that I am anything else."

"I never doubted that you were more," she told him, her voice suddenly husky.

He shook his head. "It would be a mistake not to think that I am more, Lara. I am a man—with the same wants and needs as any other man."

"Why are you telling me this?"

"To remind myself of the fact. And maybe to warn you about the same thing."

She swallowed. "Your Highness—"

"Rowan," he told her.

"It's late," she said, picking up her plate and glass to carry them to the sink. "And the children will be up early in the morning. I really should get some sleep."

"Lara?"

He could tell that she wanted to ignore him, but she paused at the door and reluctantly turned back to face him. "Yes, Your Highness?"

He studied her for a moment, noting the flushed cheeks, the twined fingers, and knew the attraction he felt wasn't entirely one-sided. But he had yet to figure out what he was going to do about it except that his decision would have to wait for another day.

"Sweet dreams," was all he said.

Chapter Seven

Michael Leandres did a double-take when he returned to his office and found his mother waiting for him. He could count on one hand the number of times she'd ventured through the doors of his company in the past five years, and he knew she wouldn't be there now unless it was important—at least to her.

He closed the door to give them some privacy and crossed the room to kiss her cheek. "This is a surprise."

She raised one perfectly arched brow. "Samantha didn't tell you that I called yesterday?"

"She did. But it was late when I got in last night, then I had an early meeting this morning, and I have another one—" he glanced at his watch as he settled into his chair "—in twenty minutes."

Elena's lips thinned. "This is important, Michael."

"I've got twenty minutes," he said again.

"Instead of wasting your talents running this company, you could be running the country."

That certainly drew his attention away from the messages waiting on his computer.

"You're a royal, Michael. You were meant for greater things than this."

"This" being the advertising company he'd built from the ground up, relying only on his education and ambition rather than the fact that he'd inherited some blue blood from his mother.

"I'm happy with my life," he told her.

"You should be on the throne."

"Rowan is the prince regent."

"For now," she agreed. "But his position is far from secure."

"What are you saying, Mother?"

"I'm just reminding you that any member of the royal family can challenge the authority of a ruler believed to be unsuitable."

"I'd imagine when parliament made that provision, it was with the expectation that there would be valid grounds for such a challenge," he pointed out.

"Obviously," she agreed, ignoring his sarcasm. "And your cousin has lived and worked in London for the past ten years. He doesn't know what the people of Tesoro del Mar want or need. How can he be the appropriate choice to rule them?"

"He's done an admirable job since Julian's death."

When she spoke again, her voice had softened a little, just enough to suggest that she understood he was grieving for the loss of a man who had been not just his cousin but one of his best friends. "I appreciate that this is a difficult situation—"

"Do you?" he interrupted to ask. "Do you understand that the whole country is mourning for Julian and Catherine and for the children who have suddenly lost both of their parents? Or is this just a chance to make a play for the crown that you always craved for yourself?"

"Only a fool would deny that this is an incredible opportunity for our family."

"Then I guess I'm a fool," he said easily. "Because I don't want any part of whatever you're planning."

"I expect your brother will feel differently."

As much as Michael loved his brother—and he did, even though they rarely saw eye to eye on anything—he couldn't imagine Cameron running a charity event never mind a country. On the other hand, that might be exactly why Elena was eager to see her youngest son in the highest office, so that she could pull the strings and advance her own agenda.

"Obviously that's something you'll have to discuss with Cameron," he said. "But I want you to know that I won't support any attempt to take the throne away from Julian's children through Rowan."

She picked up her purse. "I had hoped you would have more of a sense of family loyalty."

"They're our family, too, Mother."

But she was already out the door.

Rowan hadn't slept well since taking the throne. If it wasn't his duties that weighed on his mind, it was the inappropriate fantasies about the royal nanny that plagued his sleep or, more recently, nightmares about nameless, faceless brides. His brothers both found his marriage dilemma amusing but Rowan did not, and Henri's reassurance that there would be no shortage of women wanting to be his wife was hardly reassuring. He knew that their eagerness to wed the prince regent had more to do with his title and status than him as a person.

It shouldn't matter why a woman wanted to be his wife. After all, he wasn't looking for a love match but only to make the best of a bad situation. A situation that went from bad to worse when he entered his office early the next morning and found it already occupied.

He recognized the older woman as Helene Renaud, a member of the palace housekeeping staff, but he was certain he'd never seen the younger woman with her.

"Good morning, Your Highness." Helene curtsied as she greeted him in French.

He returned her greeting, albeit a little warily.

"This is my daughter, Jocelyn," the maid told him.

Rowan's gaze drifted to the girl by her side, for he saw now that she was a girl and probably not much older than his eldest nephew, though he was still at a loss as to what either of them was doing in his office.

"She's a pretty girl, isn't she?" Helene continued. "And she will make a beautiful bride."

A beautiful bride?

Suddenly the reason for the maid's presence—and that of her daughter—was all too clear.

"She's a very beautiful girl," he agreed. "But she's a child."

"She will be fifteen on her birthday in three weeks," Helene told him. "The paper said your bride must be fifteen."

"The paper?"

She handed him a copy of the morning paper.

It was only years of training that allowed Rowan to note the headline without any outward hint of surprise, and though his irritation increased with each word of the article he scanned, he gave no indication of such.

"Right there," the girl's mother said again, pointing a

finger at the exact part of the article where the criteria for a royal bride were enumerated.

"It says the bride must be *at least* fifteen years of age," Rowan acknowledged. "I'm looking for someone a little bit older."

"It says fifteen," she repeated.

"Because this is an ancient piece of legislation," he pointed out to her. "People got married at a lot younger age then because they died younger."

"It also says that your bride must be of moral character. Not many girls past the age of fifteen are virgins anymore," she told him. "I have another daughter, Brigitte. She is seventeen, but I cannot vouch for her innocence. I know my Jocelyn is untouched."

Rowan cast a quick glance at the young girl, who had remained silent throughout the discussion. Now her cheeks were stained with red and her eyes filled with tears, and he knew she wasn't just humiliated but terrified at the thought of being offered as a child bride.

Turning away from the mother, he stepped closer to the girl. "You will undoubtedly make a beautiful bride someday," he assured her. "But hopefully it won't be for many more years yet and it definitely shouldn't be to an old man like me."

She cast a quick, worried glance at her mother, who was scowling at their exchange.

"You are not so old," the girl protested weakly.

"But too old for you." He smiled and reached for her hands, gently prying apart the fingers that were laced so tightly together. He lifted first one, then the other, to his lips, then released them. "It was a pleasure meeting you, Miss Jocelyn, but I think you must be going now so you aren't late for school."

"Yes, Your Highness." She dropped into a quick and awkward curtsy.

"You are making a mistake," the girl's mother said.

"The mistake may be in not terminating your employment here," the prince said mildly. "And one I will rectify if you're not out of my office in the next three seconds."

The maid hurried after her daughter, and Rowan sank into the chair behind his desk.

"I'm surprised, Your Highness."

He glanced up, startled to see Lara hovering in the doorway through which the young girl and her mother had just left, and unnerved by the tug of longing her presence triggered inside him. But his voice was light when he asked, "Surprised that I threatened to fire her or that I didn't actually do so?"

"By how easily you handled the whole situation, and impressed by the compassion you showed her daughter," she said. "Helene may be disappointed that her daughter won't be the next princess of Tesoro del Mar, but the girl will always remember the prince who treated her kindly."

"I'm not in the habit of yelling at young girls," he told her.

"Good to know." She smiled, and the tug came again, a little more insistently this time. "It's true then? That you have to marry?"

He nodded. "According to Tesorian law, a ruling prince who is not wed before his thirty-fifth birthday must take a bride within six months of that date or forfeit his crown."

"Isn't the idea of a forced marriage a little...outdated?"

"More than a little," he acknowledged. "But Tesoro del Mar is a country built on history and tradition. And it is my honor and my duty to rule until Christian is of an age to take his place on the throne."

"Then Madame Renaud is probably only the first of

many who will be pushing eligible daughters in your direction." Lara glanced pointedly at the newspaper headline. "Especially when they see that 'Recipe for a Royal Bride.'"

Rowan shoved the paper aside. "Who comes up with those headlines? And what kind of woman would offer her teenage daughter as a virgin sacrifice?"

"A woman who wants a front seat at the royal wedding?"

He just shook his head. "What about what her daughter wants?"

"Some mothers are more concerned about their own needs than those of their children."

Though her tone was deliberately light, he sensed the underlying tension that hinted of some personal experience. And though his own life was in chaos right now, he found himself wanting to know more about hers, wanting to uncover all of her secrets. Maybe then he would be able to get her out of his system and concentrate his attention on finding a bride.

"Was yours like that?" he asked.

"I beg your pardon?"

"Your mother," he prompted. "Was she like Madame Renaud?"

Her smile was thin. "My mother would never have thought I was worthy of a prince."

There was definitely tension now, and a hint of both anger and sadness in those deep green eyes. But before he could question her further, she forged ahead.

"Speaking of princes," she said. "I wanted to thank you for making such an effort with Christian. I saw him this morning when he came back from riding with you, and I know he's really enjoying the time you spend with him."

"I enjoy it, too," he admitted.

"I'm glad," she said. "But you should know that now Princess Alexandria is demanding equal time."

"Meaning?"

"She wants you to join us for movie night."

"When?"

"Tonight. I told her that you probably already had plans, but she insisted that I ask you, anyway."

"Unfortunately, I do have plans."

That hint of a smile appeared again. "With the lovely young Jocelyn?"

"Please. It's a fund-raising dinner for the new wing of the children's hospital, and my date is a twenty-eight-year-old American heiress."

"Then I hope you have a good time."

He made a face. "I'll be eating rubber chicken and wishing I was watching—"

"Beauty and the Beast." Amusement danced in her eyes. "The rubber chicken doesn't seem so unappealing now, does it?"

"It's a toss-up," he admitted. "Though I seem to recall *Beauty and the Beast* is a fairly short movie while these fund-raising events go on for hours."

"I'll pass your regrets on to Lexi," she told him.

"And I'll try to see her myself before I go, but the way my day is shaping up, there's no guarantee I'll have the time."

"I won't take up any more of it."

As he watched her walk out of his office, he found himself genuinely regretting having to turn down her invitation. Movie night actually sounded like fun, and he couldn't remember having any of that in a very long time.

On the other hand, a cozy evening in front of the television with Lara might be more of a temptation than he could resist, and he couldn't afford that kind of distraction right now. He had to find a bride.

Lara was balancing on that precipice between sleep and consciousness when she realized she wasn't alone. Lifting heavy eyelids, she saw Rowan reach for the remote. With the press of a button the television screen went black, leaving the room in darkness except for the soft glow of a single lamp on the end table.

"I didn't mean to disturb you," he said when he turned and saw that she'd awakened.

It occurred to her that she should untangle her legs from the blanket and rise to curtsy, but he gestured for her to remain where she was.

"I didn't intend to fall asleep."

He smiled. "How was movie night?"

"Good. Lexi and Damon went to bed after *Beauty and the Beast,* then Christian and I watched the last *Pirates* flick, and after I made sure he'd turned out his lights and gone to sleep, I came in to clear away our drinks and snacks and got distracted by an old film that was showing on television." She was rambling, but she couldn't seem to help herself. She was disoriented from sleep and unnerved by his presence and had a tendency to talk too much when she was nervous.

"What was the movie?" He reached into the bowl on the table to grab a handful of leftover popcorn.

"An Affair to Remember."

"That is an old one."

"A classic," she countered automatically.

"Did you have movie nights when you were a kid?"

"No. Julian and Catherine started it with the children, I've just continued it."

He grabbed another handful of popcorn.

"Was the rubber chicken that bad?"

"Not as bad as I feared."

"And the American heiress?"

Rowan rolled his eyes. "Let's just say I sincerely regret missing movie night."

She laughed. "I'm sorry."

He shrugged. "On a more positive note, the hospital will get its new wing."

"That's good news, then."

"Why is it you don't like to talk about your childhood?"

"There's not much to talk about."

"Then why do you redirect the conversation whenever I try to ask any questions about your past?"

And she'd thought she was being subtle. "I just can't imagine why you'd be interested."

"The *why* aside, it seems that I am."

"Okay. What do you want to know?"

"Your mother died when you were fifteen and your father when you were too young to remember him—"

"I never said my father died." She was always clear about that, and not bothered by the fact that most people drew the same conclusion Rowan apparently had. She'd been honest with Julian and Catherine about her parentage, of course, and she owed Rowan the same courtesy. She didn't want him to stop looking at her the way he was looking at her right now—as if he was really interested, as if she was someone who truly mattered, but she couldn't perpetuate his mistaken belief. "I said I never knew him."

He considered this, his gaze unwavering, as he munched on his popcorn. "Your parents weren't married."

"That's right."

"And your mother never did marry?"

She shook her head. "She couldn't find any man who was willing to take on the burden of someone else's bastard child."

"Is that what she told you?"

"That's how it was. There were men—a lot of men—who were interested in my mother, but the interest quickly waned when they realized she came with child-size baggage." She picked up her now-flat soda and sipped.

"I'm starting to understand why you don't like to talk about it."

She shrugged. "It was a long time ago."

"Not so long," he said. "Though I have to wonder how a child so obviously unappreciated by her mother could grow into a woman so warm and caring and generous."

She felt her skin grow warm beneath his gaze and was suddenly aware that it was late, and he wasn't turning away from her despite the revelations she'd made. She swallowed another mouthful of her lukewarm drink.

"After my mother died, I was put in foster care. After a few months Stephanie and David Mitchell showed up at the door. Stephanie was my mother's second cousin, David was her husband, and for some reason they wanted me to live with them. Social services was more than happy to unload me, and within a few days, I was on a plane to Ireland.

"Actually," she continued, "it's because of David that I met your brother and sister-in-law. As it turned out, his sister's husband was Catherine's uncle."

"I never realized there was a familial connection," Rowan said.

"A distant and tenuous one."

"So how did you end up in Tesoro del Mar?"

"Catherine asked me to come."

"It couldn't have been that simple."

"It wasn't an easy decision to make," she agreed. "Stephanie was more of a mother to me than mine had ever been, and David was like the father I never had, but I was almost twenty-one years old, ready to start living my own life, and it seemed like a good opportunity."

"No regrets?"

She shook her head, unwilling to admit to him that she did have one—falling for a man who could never be hers.

As Rowan trudged up the wide staircase toward his apartment on the fourth floor six days later, he couldn't help but resent the seemingly endless social engagements that stretched ahead of him over the next few weeks. As if his usual 101 daily responsibilities weren't enough, he was somehow supposed to find the time to choose a bride and plan a wedding. The rare free evenings that he'd enjoyed prior to learning of parliament's mandate had become a thing of the past, and though tonight had only been his fourth date, he was already tired of the process.

After the fund-raising dinner with the American heiress last week, there had been a performance of the national ballet with a photographer who claimed a distant connection to Italian royalty, then a charity ball with a widowed countess who had clearly married the first time for wealth and status and was prepared to do so again. Then tonight's fund-raising dinner with the admittedly lovely but uninspiring Stacy Phillips.

All of the women had been attractive, and certainly they all satisfied the criteria enumerated for a royal bride, but not one of them intrigued him enough to want to spend a second night in her company, never mind the rest of his life.

He wanted someone he could feel comfortable enough

with to put his feet up and watch a movie, or share quiet conversation and a slice of leftover cake in the kitchen long after everyone else had gone to sleep. Someone he could talk to about the things that really mattered and the things that didn't. Someone who would share her own opinions, even if that opinion was that he was acting like an arrogant pompous ass.

He wanted, in a word, Lara.

Beyond the physical attraction that he'd felt from the beginning, he found that the more time he spent with her the more he genuinely liked her. She was smart and kind with a generous heart and a surprising sense of humor. She made him smile when he hadn't had anything to smile about in a long time. And she made him wonder—about the taste of her lips, the scent of her skin and the sensation of her naked flesh against his own. Definitely not anything he should be wondering about when he had a country to run and a wedding to plan.

He stifled a yawn as he started up past the nursery. All he wanted to do now was fall into bed and sleep until morning. A quick glance at his watch warned that morning wasn't so very far away. Well, a few hours' sleep would have to do. He'd been existing on no more than that for several weeks now.

He paused with his foot on the step and strained to listen more closely to the sound that had caught his attention. Was that…singing?

He turned left instead of right and made his way down the hall. As he did, the sound became more audible.

He realized that he was hearing the song Alexandria had told him about—the lullaby that Catherine used to sing to her children and that Lara now sang whenever they had bad dreams.

He paused outside the door of his young nephew's bedroom and listened as the soft lyrical voice wrapped around him, captivating him like the soft shimmering threads of a magical web.

The room was lit only by the glow of the half-moon outside the window, but it was enough to illuminate her silhouette as she sat on the edge of the mattress rubbing Damon's back as the song lulled him back to sleep.

Something stirred inside him, an unfamiliar feeling that was somehow both gentle and compelling.

Lara backed toward the door, the words fading to a soft hum as she tiptoed away from the sleeping child. When she stepped over the threshold and turned into him, he reached out automatically to steady her. She gasped softly as his hands settled on her narrow hips.

Her head tipped back, her eyes widened.

She tried to draw away, but now that he finally had her in his arms, he found he wasn't ready to release her so soon.

He could feel the warmth of her skin through the thin barrier of fabric, and he could all too easily imagine untying the knot and slipping the garment from her shoulders. He wanted to discover what she wore beneath, and then he wanted to strip that away, as well. He wanted to explore the soft feminine curves of her naked body with his hands and his lips and—

"Your Highness?"

The question drew his attention back.

He watched her throat move as she swallowed, then the tip of her tongue came out to moisten her lips.

There was only so much temptation a man could be expected to resist, and he'd been resisting too long already.

He pulled her tight against his body and dipped his head to cover her mouth with his own.

Chapter Eight

Shock held Lara frozen for the first few seconds. Then the heat of Rowan's embrace seeped through the numbness and everything inside her simply melted.

If she'd been able to think clearly—heck, if she'd been able to think at all—she might have been annoyed by his arrogant assumption that he could take what he wanted just because he was a prince. But her brain seemed to have short-circuited the minute his lips touched hers, and she was lost in the mindlessness of a long-burning passion finally acknowledged.

His mouth was hot and hungry, not coaxing a response but demanding it. And she was helpless to do anything but respond. Maybe it wasn't the gentle kiss she might have dreamed about, that her naive heart yearned for, but it was Rowan kissing her, and that was all that mattered.

His hands were hard and bold as they moved over her

body, and she burned everywhere that he touched. They slid from her shoulders, down her back, over the curve of her buttocks to pull her more tightly against him. She could feel his arousal against the throbbing heat between her thighs and instinctively pressed herself even closer.

He groaned—a raw expression of need that somehow echoed the desperate churning deep inside herself. She held nothing back from him as she returned his kiss with a passion she'd never experienced before. Her lips parted willingly to the searching thrust of his tongue as she lifted her arms to wind them around his neck. Her breasts rubbed against the hard wall of his chest, her pebbled nipples straining against the thin layers of clothing that separated them from more intimate contact.

A quick tug untied the knot of her robe so that it fell open, and then his hands were on her breasts, his thumbs stroking boldly over the aching peaks so that she gasped with shocked pleasure as arrows of heat speared to her center.

"You are so damn beautiful." The words were a ragged whisper against her mouth as his hands continued to explore her curves through the thin cotton. "So damn tempting."

She didn't know how to respond to that, so she said nothing. Instead she let her instincts guide her and nipped at the sexy curve of his bottom lip.

His hands had found the hem of her nightdress and dipped beneath, the stroke of his broad palms over her bare skin making her tremble and ache with wanting.

Her heart was pounding, her blood was racing, and her body was aching for something she wasn't entirely sure she understood but somehow knew he could give her.

She wasn't completely innocent. She'd been on dates and she'd been kissed, but never had she been kissed like this. Never had she experienced anything that even hinted at such all-consuming passion.

His hands continued to move over her, light touches and bold strokes that made her tremble and quiver and want. His lips slid away from hers to skim across her cheek, down her neck, then lower still. His mouth covered her breast, and she gasped. His lips closed around the peaked nipple, his tongue laved, and she moaned. She could feel the moist heat of his mouth through the thin barrier of fabric, and she instinctively arched, her fingers sliding through his hair to hold his head at her breast.

She hadn't realized that she could feel so much or want so desperately. She'd never expected that her blood could pulse so hot and fast through her veins that it seemed to melt everything inside of her.

Then his hand slipped between her thighs, touching her where no one had ever touched her before, and sparks danced and skipped toward her center. His fingers moved in a gentle circular motion, caressing her through her panties, and her hips moved in an instinctive and unconscious rhythmic response.

She barely registered the throaty murmurs that originated somewhere deep inside her, didn't understand the breathless pleas that tumbled from her lips. There was no sense of time or place—there was only Rowan and a fierce and aching need to be with him. A need that continued to build, an unfamiliar tension escalating deep inside, winding her tighter, spiraling her higher, until she was afraid that she might shatter—and more afraid that she wouldn't.

Suddenly he grasped her shoulders, no longer gentle—the fire in his eyes was more fury than passion now as he shoved her away from him, his fingers biting into her flesh as he held her at arm's length.

"Damn it, Lara, when were you going to tell me to stop?"

She tried to draw a breath, to unscramble the jumble of chaotic emotions that continued to course through her system and understand what had caused him to pull away from her. But her mind was still floating in a misty fog of delirium, unwilling to accept his abrupt withdrawal.

"I don't want you to stop," she admitted breathlessly. "I want you to kiss me again. I want you to touch me."

He dropped his hands and stepped back, shaking his head. "Are you really so naive that you don't know where this is heading? Or so shameless you don't care?"

She pressed a hand to her chest, as if the gesture might settle the frantic pounding of her heart. She felt chilled all of a sudden, cold without the heat of his body against hers, and colder still when she finally registered the scorn in his dark brown eyes.

How could he kiss her with such passion one moment and glower at her with such disapproval the next? What had she done—or not done—to cause this change in his mood?

She started to speak, to apologize, then stopped short, not sure what she was supposed to be apologizing for. "*You* kissed *me*," she finally said. "So why are you acting as if I did something wrong?"

"Because you—*we*—shouldn't have let things go as far as they did. I could have taken you, right here in the middle of the hall outside of my nephew's bedroom, and you wouldn't have done anything to stop me, would you?"

She wished she had an easy response to dismiss what had happened between them as readily as he had done, but she wasn't that experienced or sophisticated and she wasn't going to lie to him.

"I don't know," she admitted, fumbling as she reached for the belt of her robe. "I didn't think about where we were or what was happening. I couldn't think. When you kissed me, when you touched me—it was like my mind just shut off. I've never felt like that before."

His eyes narrowed. "What do you mean—you've never felt like that before?"

Where she'd been cold only moments before, the intensity of his gaze had her cheeks flushing again, though the heat was from embarrassment rather than desire this time.

"I mean that no one has ever kissed me like that, or touched me the way you touched me."

When she finally managed to knot the belt and looked up at him again, she found he was staring at her.

"You can't be a virgin," he said flatly.

She wouldn't have thought it possible, but her face flamed even hotter. "You didn't approve of me when you thought I was a woman of loose morals, and now you seem to disapprove of my inexperience."

"Let's clarify that," he said carefully. "Are you telling me that you have little experience…or no experience?"

"I've been kissed before."

Rowan frowned at her.

"Kissed," he echoed disbelievingly.

Her chin lifted. "I'm not going to apologize for not sleeping around."

"No one is asking you to apologize," he told her.

"Then why are you angry with me?"

He scrubbed his hands over his face. "I'm angry at myself," he finally admitted. "For not realizing you were innocent."

"You think you should have known?" she challenged.

"Yes." He caught her gaze, held it. "And even now, even

knowing that you are untouched—*Mi Dios*—I can't help but want you still."

Her heart pounded, her throat went dry. "You still... want me?"

"I've wanted you for a long time," he admitted. "And even knowing that I shouldn't have let things go as far as they did, I can't seem to stop wanting you."

"I haven't been saving myself," she told him. "I just never met anyone who made me want to take a physical relationship to the next level—until you."

He took a careful and deliberate step away from her. "You're even more innocent than I guessed if you don't realize what an admission like that can do to a man."

"Tell me," she said.

He shook his head, knowing she would be impossible to resist if she had any hint of the power she had over him.

"Go to your room and lock the door, Lara," he said instead.

She took a step toward him, then another. "I'm not afraid of you, Your Highness."

"I would think, under the circumstances, that you could dispense with my title," he said wryly.

Though her cheeks flushed, her gaze never wavered. "I'm not afraid of you...Rowan."

It was the first time he'd ever heard her speak his name, and the way she said it now—a soft, husky whisper on lips that were erotically swollen from his kisses—was unbearably arousing.

He tried to remember that she was more than a beautiful young woman ripe for seduction—she was an employee of the royal household, the nanny deeply loved by his brother's children, and she was innocent. It was that last thought that helped him snap a tight leash on his raging desire, and instead of dragging her into his arms to pick up where they left off, he touched a gentle hand to her cheek. "It would be better for both of us if you were."

"Why?"

"Because I have only five months left to find a bride," he said, his hand dropping away as he reminded both of them of this fact, "and I can't let myself be distracted from that task."

She nodded her agreement. "Of course, Your Highness."

His smile was wry. "We're back to the title again, are we?"

"I think it's wise." She dipped into a curtsy. "Good night."

"Good night, Lara."

Rowan watched her disappear into her own room, listening for the telltale click after the door closed behind her. But she didn't slide the lock into place, and he couldn't help but wonder if it was because she trusted him to act honorably or because she didn't want him to.

Turning away from the temptation, he went to his rooms and took a very cold shower.

As the icy water pounded against his skin, he tried to clear his mind of all thoughts of Lara. But he could still taste the flavor of her kiss, feel the satin smoothness of her skin, and hear her throaty sighs. His body was almost numb with the cold when he finally shut off the spray— but his blood was still pulsing with need.

He yanked a towel from the heated bar and damned himself for being such a fool.

He should have learned his lesson years ago, should have heeded the warning bells that sounded in his head the first time he set eyes on her. He'd experienced the same type of immediate and intense attraction only once before and had soon regretted allowing himself to be seduced by the temptation of Margot Olivier.

He'd just started college when they met. She was the teaching assistant for his first-year philosophy course, three years his senior, worldly, sophisticated and stunningly beautiful. He'd been instantly smitten, and when she'd told him she loved him, he believed her.

It had taken him almost two years to realize she loved the perks of being a royal girlfriend more than she loved him. She'd used his title to gain them access to the most popular dance clubs and entertainment venues, and Rowan had been so happy to be with her, he hadn't cared. Until it got to the point where she seemed to be partying all the time, drinking more than she could handle, experimenting with drugs. He tried to get her to stop, but she accused him of being a spoilsport.

He finally walked away, convinced that she would give up her dangerous lifestyle when she realized it was tearing them apart. She didn't even notice until the time came when she needed him to bail her out of trouble and he was no longer around.

That was when she'd told him she was pregnant.

He'd been stunned and terrified but determined to do the right thing. Then he found out she'd even lied about carrying his baby, and he realized he had done the right thing when he walked away from her the first time.

Of course, he'd been a lot younger then, a lot more susceptible. And Margot had been a master manipulator. She'd enticed and seduced, using his desire for her to get what she wanted. In the end, she'd left him not so much brokenhearted as disillusioned. And determined to never make the same mistake again.

He didn't really believe that Lara was anything like

Margot. He didn't think she could fake her sweetness and innocence—or the confusion and hurt that had shone in her eyes when he'd sent her away.

He'd berated her for almost letting herself be taken in the hallway, but he was the one who'd almost taken her there. He'd been so wrapped up in the passion of their kiss that he hadn't cared about anything but assuaging the violent need churning in his blood.

If he hadn't managed to hang on to that one last shred of decency, he might have laid her down on the antique carpet or pressed her up against the silk-covered walls without a thought for anything but burying himself in her hot body.

And he couldn't help but think he'd be feeling a hell of a lot better right now if he had.

Lara needed to get away from the palace. She often used her day off to catch up on homework, but she'd finished her last assignment and written her last exam, so she actually had free time for a change. She considered taking one of the horses for a ride or lazing by the pool with a good book, but both of those possibilities carried with them the risk of running into Rowan, and she wasn't quite ready to face him again.

She had no idea what his plans were for the day. He might be on his way out of the country for all she knew, but after last night, she wasn't going to hang around to find out.

Rowan might have made the first move, but she'd matched him step for step after that. Not just a willing participant but an eager one. There was no denying the way she had responded to his kiss, his touch. He'd stirred wants and needs inside her that she hadn't imagined.

And in the light of day, though she might be embarrassed by what had happened between them, ashamed by her wanton behavior, she was unable to deny that there was a part of her that wished he hadn't stopped. Not that she really wanted him to make love with her in the middle of the hallway, but she really wanted him to make love with her.

As much as she wished he hadn't stopped, she knew that an affair with the prince would only lead to heartache. She'd yet to offer either her body or her heart to a man, and she feared that she couldn't share the former without also sacrificing the latter. Or maybe she already had.

It was a thought that niggled at her on her way into town and continued to worry her as she wandered through the market and browsed in the shops. Though she usually loved visiting Port Augustine with its little boutiques and sidewalk cafés, as she found herself navigating through crowds of tourists doing the same thing, she found her heart just wasn't in it today.

Deciding company and conversation were what she needed rather than solitary brooding, she turned toward the art gallery. She found Tanis finishing up a tour and tagged along for the end of it. When Tanis had answered the last question and said goodbye to the last visitor, she turned to Lara with a bright, if somewhat weary, smile.

"That's my fourth group already today and let me tell you, these shoes are not as comfortable as the salesman promised they'd be." Tan twisted the cap off a bottle of water and took a long swallow. "Of course, it would help if I'd remembered that it was Wednesday before I put them on this morning."

Lara glanced at the sleek ivory slingbacks on her friend's feet. "Because those are definitely Friday shoes."

Tan rolled her eyes. "Because Wednesday is cruise ship

day, and the tourists usually like a little cultural education to add to their shopping experience."

"And soon they'll be looking at your work in here," she pointed out.

For months Lara had been urging her friend to show her paintings to the gallery owner, but Tanis had been reluctant to do so. When she and Luke recently became lovers, she had become adamant in her refusal. But fate had taken a hand, leading Luke to discover some canvases she'd hidden in the back of a closet. He'd been so impressed that he'd immediately starting planning for her show.

Tanis smiled now at Lara's reference to the event. "Okay, that'll help me get through the day even if it won't make my feet feel better—or help us to get a seat at The Angel."

"We can do take-out," Lara suggested.

So they went to their favorite café where patrons were lined up waiting for tables and ordered sandwiches and sodas to go. They carried their lunches down to the pier to eat while watching the boats on the water.

"What are you doing in town today?" Tan asked.

"I just needed a change of scenery."

"I imagine those ivory towers must seem monotonous after a while."

Lara ignored her sarcasm as she unwrapped her sandwich.

"So what did he do?" Tan prompted.

"Who?"

"His Royal Arrogance, of course. Even on your day off, you don't like to be too far away from the children in case they need you for anything, so something must have happened to make you want to avoid their guardian."

She should have known that her friend would guess

something was up—or maybe that was why she'd come here. She desperately needed someone else's perspective and Tanis was the only person she trusted with her deepest secrets. So she took a deep breath and said, "He kissed me."

"And…"

"And I melted," Lara admitted. "I never understood what that meant, until he took me in his arms and everything inside me turned to mush."

Tanis frowned as she chewed on her straw. "I knew this would happen if you went back there."

"Knew what would happen?"

"That you would fall in love with him."

"I'm not—" Lara huffed out a breath when Tanis's eyebrows lifted. "I like him."

"Yeah, there's a newsflash," her friend said drily.

"I mean, above and beyond the fact that he's gorgeous and a prince, I actually like who he is."

"But he's a prince."

"I know he's way out of my league," she admitted. "And I'm not naive enough to actually fantasize about having a relationship with him. I just want to be with him—even once. Just to finally know what it's like to be with a man."

Tanis nearly choked on her soda. Setting her drink aside, she stared at her friend. "You're not still a virgin."

Lara felt her cheeks flush as she glanced furtively around to make sure no one had overhead her friend's comment. "Why does everyone keep saying that?"

"Ohmygod. You *are* still a virgin."

"So?"

"So how did I not know this?"

"Because I refuse to wear a scarlet *V* on my shirt?"

"Okay—I'm sorry. I just didn't realize—I mean, you dated. Lots of guys. Great guys. And I just assumed—"

Tan shook her head. "Obviously I assumed wrong. Never mind. The important thing to know is that you can*not* sleep with Rowan."

"I can't?"

"Definitely not. Not for your first time, anyway."

Lara frowned. "You're saying that I can sleep with Rowan if I sleep with someone else first?"

"Sure. Because a woman—maybe a man, too, though I couldn't attest to that—tends to romanticize her first sexual experience. Even if it's a fumbling, groping three-minute initiation in the backseat of a borrowed station wagon, it will forever be remembered as her first. And when that first experience is with a man who is so much more than most other men, she's doomed to a lifetime of disappointment because no one else will ever be able to measure up."

"Well, it's a moot point, anyway, because Rowan made it clear that he's too busy searching for a bride to be distracted by me."

Tanis winced in sympathy. "Then it's true—the reports in the paper about the prince regent having to get married?"

Lara tossed the remnants of her sandwich to a bird. "Yep. According to the mandate of parliament, a married ruler is more mature and responsible, understands the value of family and is better able to anticipate the needs of his people."

Tanis shook her head. "And I bet the women will line up for the chance to play his dutiful wife."

"You have no idea," Lara told her. "Mail has been coming in from all over the world—bags full every day. Everything from handwritten letters spritzed with perfume to formal résumés outlining wifely qualifications to nude photos obviously intended to appeal to his baser instincts."

"And you know this how?"

"Henri asked me to help him sort through the mail. He thought a woman's perspective would be useful."

"And you agreed?"

"What was I supposed to do?"

"Say 'Sorry, not my job.'" Tanis glanced at her watch, obviously remembering that she had to get back to hers.

Lara rose with her friend. "But the fact is, whoever Rowan chooses to marry will effectively become a step-mother to the children."

"And it doesn't bother you to be enlisted in the search for a bride for the man you dream about sleeping with?"

She just shrugged, pretending a nonchalance she didn't feel as she dropped her empty cup and wrapper in the garbage. "You told me I can't sleep with him."

"Make sure you don't forget it," Tanis warned.

Cameron Leandres poured himself another glass of Scotch before returning to his seat across from his mother. Though he was intrigued by her plan, he had some reservations about its chances for success.

"What did Michael think about all of this?" he asked Elena.

"This isn't about Michael—it's about you."

"In other words, he didn't want any part of your scheme," he guessed.

"He doesn't have your passion, Cameron. Or your ambition."

The possibility of ruling the country definitely appealed to him. He was tired of being second-rate royalty—a man with a title but no real power or wealth. Now his mother was offering him the chance for more. If her plan worked, it would change his life, his future, everything.

"What, specifically, did you have in mind?" he asked her.

"I thought a nice little scandal would be sufficient grounds for a motion of nonconfidence."

"Except that cousin Rowan isn't generally known for his scandalous behavior," he felt compelled to point out.

"Have you forgotten about Margot Olivier?"

The name didn't mean anything to him.

"That's right," she said, waving a hand dismissively. "I keep forgetting you're ten years younger than Rowan. You would have been a child, away at boarding school at the time."

"Still, it couldn't have been too much of a scandal if I never heard about it."

"It might have been huge," she said. "Except that it happened here on the island, so Eduardo managed to hush it up pretty quickly. But I was there when Rowan got the phone call that dragged him away from a formal dinner at the palace and when he returned a few hours later. And I overheard him telling his father that Margot had been arrested."

"The prince's girlfriend in prison." Cameron smiled. "Yes, that would be a scandal."

"It gets better," Elena told him. "When Eduardo insisted that her wild behavior proved she was an unsuitable companion for a member of the royal family, Rowan confided that she was pregnant."

His heart pounded with excitement. "If Rowan has an illegitimate child, that's immediate grounds for disqualification."

"Yes, well, unfortunately Margot lied about that little fact."

The excitement faded. "It wasn't Rowan's child?"

"She wasn't even pregnant, but she knew that claiming she was having his baby was the one thing that might get him back after he'd realized she wanted the status of being with a royal more than she wanted him and severed their relationship. And he might have fallen for it, if Eduardo hadn't stepped in and insisted on having her examined by the royal doctor to ensure she and the baby were in good health after their ordeal. His examination confirmed that there was no baby."

Cameron could only imagine how humiliating that revelation had been for his cousin, but he didn't allow himself to feel any sympathy. As far as he was concerned, everything had always come too easily for the Santiago brothers and Rowan was no exception. It was time for the Leandres family to have some of the fame and fortune and a place in the history books of Tesoro del Mar.

"How is this supposed to help us now?" he asked his mother. "A decade-old scandal isn't likely to sway public opinion."

"We could find Margot, bring her back—"

He shook his head. "Do you really believe, after more than a dozen years, that Rowan has any feelings for her?"

"Well, as far as I know, he's never been seriously involved with anyone else since then."

"Because he's wary, not brokenhearted," Cameron assured her.

"Do you have a better idea?"

He swallowed the last mouthful of Scotch. "As a matter of fact, I do."

Chapter Nine

She was missing an earring.

It wasn't normally the type of thing that would send Lara into a panic, but it wasn't her usual gold hoops that she'd been wearing. She grabbed her ear, felt the familiar shape and texture of the one teardrop-shaped topaz surrounded by tiny diamonds. Where was the other one?

She ran her hands over the surface of the dressing table, as if her hands might find what her eyes couldn't see, but without success. She'd put them both in—she was sure of it. In fact, she'd just finished doing so when Lexi came running to tell her that Damon was climbing up the bookcases in the library…

She slipped her feet into her shoes and hurried down to the library.

He'd grinned at her from his precarious perch on the edge of a shelf that was taller than she was, and when she'd demanded that he get down immediately, he'd jumped to her, completely fearless. She'd caught him, hugging him close, though she'd been sorely tempted to paddle his bottom to ensure he wouldn't pull such a daredevil stunt again. And she suspected that somewhere in that process, he'd knocked her earring out.

She walked directly into the room, not hearing Rowan's voice until she'd crossed the threshold. He was hanging up the phone, obviously just having finished a call, and she curtsied automatically.

"I beg your pardon, Your Highness." She started to back out of the room.

"No need," he told her, rising to his feet. "My call is finished."

"I just wanted to take a quick look around," she told him. "I was in here earlier and may have lost—"

"This?" he asked, pulling the topaz teardrop from his pocket.

Her relief was immediate. "Yes. Thank you."

He came around the desk, studying the earring he held between his thumb and forefinger. "A gift from someone special?"

"Yes." She held out her hand, but he made no move to relinquish the gem.

"A boyfriend?" he queried.

"Does it matter?"

"I'm curious."

"David gave them to me." She'd told him about David and Stephanie, how they'd taken her back to Ireland with them after her mother passed away. Not that she expected Rowan to remember those details, nor did she intend to offer more of an explanation than she'd already given.

"David Mitchell?" he asked, surprising her with this proof that he did recall their conversation.

"Yes."

"They look like they could be family heirlooms."

"They originally belonged to his mother, who gave them to Stephanie when she married David, and when Stephanie passed away, he gave them to me. May I have it back now?"

"Of course," he said, but instead of handing it to her, he reached up and tucked her hair behind her ear, exposing the naked lobe.

She held herself perfectly still, discomfited by the intimacy of the touch, by his nearness. "I can do that."

"I'm sure you can."

But he performed the task for her, easily and efficiently, while she held her breath and prayed he wouldn't guess how his gentle touch affected her.

"They suit you." His fingers trailed down to the chain she wore around her neck and the matching topaz pendant that nestled against her throat. "Pretty. Feminine. Unique."

"Thank you." She wished he would step away, so she could breathe. But he remained where he was, so close she could feel the heat emanating from him—heat that threatened to melt everything inside of her.

"You don't often wear jewelry," he noted.

"It's not practical when I'm with the children."

"Obviously you're not going out with them tonight."

"No," she agreed. "I'm going to the opening of a new exhibit at the art gallery."

"That's right—it's your friend Tanis's work, isn't it?"

She was startled, not just that he was aware of the show but the featured artist.

"The Santiago family has long been a supporter of the

arts," he answered her unspoken question. "In fact, I was thinking that Chantal and I might check out the exhibit a little bit later this evening."

She forced a smile, as if she were pleased that he was seeing Chantal St. Laurent again. And she knew she should be, because the sooner the prince decided on a bride, the sooner she might stop fantasizing that he could ever be interested in a woman without an appropriate pedigree. A woman like her.

She deliberately stepped away, irritated that she could be so susceptible to his casual touches and easy charm when he was only toying with her. What else could it be when he had a French supermodel waiting in the wings?

"This is your second date with Ms. St. Laurent?" she asked.

He nodded.

"Then things must be going well."

"She can hold up her end of a conversation," he said.

Lara frowned. "That's hardly a ringing endorsement."

He shrugged. "In addition to fitting the criteria, she's attractive, she isn't bothered by public scrutiny, and she doesn't bore me."

"High praise," she said drily. "You might consider having those words written into your wedding vows."

She saw the gleam of amusement in the dark-chocolate eyes that met hers. "Why are you offended?"

"Because you should want more for yourself, and more from the woman you're going to marry."

"I'm marrying for duty, not desire," he reminded her.

"Another point I'm sure you've made clear to the numerous women vying to be chosen as your bride."

"The woman I choose to marry will be honored and cherished and she will never have any cause to doubt that."

"What about loved?"

He shook his head. "You're innocent in more ways than I even realized."

"We're not talking about me, we're talking about your future wife."

"Do you really think any of the women participating in this mockery of a courtship are looking to fall in love? They don't want me—they want the title and crown of Princess of Tesoro del Mar."

"Maybe that's not so unreasonable, since you just want to satisfy the mandate of parliament."

A muscle in his jaw flexed. "What I want hardly matters. I'm doing what must be done for the future of the monarchy in this country."

"Then you do want something more?"

"Of course I do. But I can't have what I want."

"How do you know?" she challenged. "Why are you so convinced of that?"

His eyes locked on hers. "Because I want you, Lara."

And she could tell by the naked desire she saw in his gaze that it was true. The realization both thrilled and terrified her. She feared he would see the same want in her own eyes, but she was helpless to look away, unable to hide her feelings or guard her heart.

"I want to make love with you. Slowly. Sweetly. And thoroughly. I want to touch you and taste you and hear you call out my name." He cupped her face in his hands, and she was trapped, not so much by his hands as by the hypnotic intensity of his words. "Say it, Lara. Say my name."

She couldn't refuse. In that moment, she couldn't have refused him anything. She moistened her lips with her tongue, conscious of the pounding of her heart, the pulsing of her blood, then whispered, "Rowan."

It was all she managed before his mouth crushed down on hers.

If he could have nothing else, Rowan would have this— a kiss, a moment, a memory. And he took it, knowing that it was all he would ever have, and damning the fate that made it so.

She met his passion with her own, her avid and eager response fueling the flames of a desire that was already burning out of control.

He wanted her in his bed—that was a truth he'd recognized almost from the start. The fact that he cared about her was a more recent revelation, and a much more unnerving one. The desire to mate was a simple and primal response to an attraction and one that he'd not hesitated to act upon in the past. But to be intimate with a woman he cared about as much as he desired her was much more complicated—and much more dangerous. Especially with his own wedding in the not-too-distant future.

He'd dated a lot of beautiful women in the past few weeks, but none who lingered in his mind or stirred his blood. None who made him want as she did.

And he did want her. Even before he'd looked up to find her in the doorway, he'd been thinking about her, as he so often found himself doing these days. Then suddenly she was there, and his heart had actually skipped a beat.

He'd always thought she was beautiful. But tonight— *Mi Dios*—she was breathtaking. It wasn't the gown, though the dress looked as if it had been made for her. The bronze color highlighted the creamy tone of her skin, while the neckline was low enough to entice, the slit up the side high enough to tantalize. And the shimmery fabric caressed her curves as he dreamed of doing.

But for now, he was content just to kiss her. He felt

as if he could drown in the sweet flavor of her lips, the warm softness of her embrace, and when her lips parted and her tongue touched his, he wanted only to go on kissing her forever.

Unfortunately, the sound of footsteps in the hall put an end to that fantasy, and he reluctantly eased his lips from hers.

"Miss Chantal St. Laurent is here, Your Highness."

If the butler was aware that he'd interrupted something, he certainly gave no indication of it.

"She's waiting in the parlor," he continued.

"Thank you, Antonio."

He bowed, then backed out of the room, leaving them alone again.

Lara turned away and plucked a tissue from the box on the table, then handed it to him. "You'll want to wipe off that lipstick before you greet your guest."

"Lara—"

"I promised to check on Lexi and Damon before I left," she interrupted. "I need to do that now, or I'm going to be late."

He could order her to stay, but he wasn't sure what he'd intended to say. He didn't have the words to express the feelings that were churning inside, and even if he did, what difference could they make? He'd already taken more from her than he had any right to take. Besides, Chantal was waiting.

"I'll see you later, then," he finally said, and let her go.

Luke had outdone himself with respect to the gala. Whether it was simply his talent for putting on a show or his confidence in Tanis's work, every piece was spectacularly displayed.

Lara spent a few minutes talking to her friend and admiring the ring Luke had put on her finger only a few hours earlier—because he wanted her to be assured that he'd fallen in love with her before she proved to be a huge success. Then Lara let Tanis mingle with other guests while she took a quick tour through the exhibit and tried not to envy her best friend the success and happiness she so deserved.

Later she would wonder if it was her preoccupation with Tanis's upcoming wedding that distracted her from watching the clock or the rumbling of her stomach when the waiters started to circulate with hors d'oeuvres, but whatever her reasons, she didn't manage to escape from the gallery before the prince and his date showed up.

She couldn't have missed Rowan's entrance if she wanted to. The excited whispers that raced through the crowd and the flurry of flashbulbs that winked in the muted light attested to the fact that the prince regent had arrived. And the stunning woman who walked in with him was as accustomed to the media spotlight as any member of the royal family.

Chantal St. Laurent wasn't just the image of Divine Cosmetics, she was the face that had graced more magazine covers than any other in the past two years. She was twenty-two years old with big blue eyes, pouty lips and a figure that made men stop in their tracks.

As Lara watched the model make her way through the crowd, she couldn't help but envy her—not for her beauty or reputation but for the fact that she was with the prince tonight.

She'd given up trying to sort out her feelings for Rowan. Her emotions were too much of a tangle. She respected and admired the prince, and she'd grown to care deeply about the man behind the crown. But it hurt, more than a little, that he could kiss her as he had in the library, then carry on with his evening in the company of another woman as if the kiss had never happened.

Or maybe it had simply meant more to her than it had to him. Maybe the kiss hadn't been anything special. Maybe he'd kissed a hundred women just like that before and would kiss Chantal St. Laurent the same way later tonight.

Yes, Rowan might desire her, but he would never love her as she was starting to love him, and he could certainly never marry a palace employee. That thought was just the jolt of reality she needed to remember that she had no business dreaming of princes or fairy tales.

Then she turned, and he was there.

He smiled, and her heart pounded.

"Your friend is very talented," Rowan noted.

"Yes, she is," Lara agreed, relieved that her voice remained strong though everything inside her was weak. "But she'll be pleased to know that you think so."

"Has she forgiven me yet for trying to replace you as the royal nanny?"

"She might, after tonight. Your appearance here, and with Chantal St. Laurent, is certain to generate even more publicity for her show." She stepped away from him, all too conscious of his nearness as the eyes of all other patrons followed him around the room. "Where is your date, anyway?"

"Around."

She lifted her eyebrows at his vague response. "Shouldn't you be with her—you know, dating?"

"She doesn't need me to hold her hand every minute," he said.

Across the room Chantal was looking at them, rather than the art on display, and the narrow-eyed gaze she focused on Lara was anything but pleasant. "You should be with her."

"Chantal can take care of herself," he said. "I'm more concerned about you."

"There's no need to be concerned about me, Your Highness."

He took a step closer, so that his arm brushed against hers. She held herself still, willed herself not to respond to the casual contact, but she couldn't prevent the shivers that danced down her spine and raised goose bumps on her flesh.

"Do you want me to apologize for kissing you earlier?"

"There's no need for that, either," she told him. "I'd prefer to just forget it ever happened."

"I'm not sure I can do that," he told her. "I've been haunted by the taste of your lips since our first kiss, though I tried to convince myself the flavor couldn't possibly be as intoxicating as I remembered. Then I kissed you again, and realized that it was even more so."

She swallowed. "There are a lot of people in this room who would give almost anything for a minute of your time. You'll give them cause to gossip if you spend too many of those minutes with me."

"Then we'll finish this conversation later, Lara."

Her only response was to curtsy. "Good evening, Your Highness."

He made his way back to his date, and Lara assured herself, despite the ache in her heart, that she was glad she'd had this opportunity to see him with Chantal. Nothing like coming face-to-face with a gorgeous supermodel to remind Lara how far out of her league Rowan really was.

And though she would have avoided it if she could, she did end up face-to-face with Chantal. Lara was looking for Tanis to say good-night to her friend, when Rowan's date fell into step beside her.

"I have just one question," Chantal said to her.

Lara feigned polite interest. "What's that?"

"Are you sleeping with him?"

She paused with her wineglass halfway to her lips. "Excuse me?"

"I'm neither gullible nor stupid, and I've seen the way Rowan looks at you." Though her tone was deliberately mild, Chantal's eyes were as sharp and cold as shards of ice.

"I'm flattered that you think he could be interested in someone like me," she said.

"He's a man," the model noted derisively, "and they aren't always discriminating when it comes to sex. I just wanted to remind you that the prince might take you to his bed, but he'll never take you as his wife. And as soon as he and I are married, you'll be gone."

She managed to hold her glass steady as she lifted it in a mock toast. "Just one more reason I should hope he marries Lady Victoria Barrow then."

"Victoria?" Chantal fairly sneered the name. "He'd be bored to tears in a week with her."

"You think so?" Lara shrugged and took a bracing sip of her wine. "And yet, the prince has spent time with her on a few occasions over the past several weeks."

Chantal shrugged one bare shoulder. "I'm not worried about Victoria. After all, I'm here with him now." Her lips curved with supreme self-confidence. "And I'm the one who will be with him tonight."

And with that parting remark, she sauntered away, leaving Lara both shaken and seething.

She stayed another half hour, so she didn't look as if she was in retreat. Then she said goodbye to Tanis and went home.

* * *

Lara had gone.

She'd slipped away, not without Rowan being aware of her departure but unable to do anything about it. He'd seen her talking briefly to Chantal, and then, before he could end his conversation with Luke Kerrigan, she was on her way to the door. He wished he could have slipped away with her.

"Looking for someone?" Chantal whispered the question close to his ear.

He forced a smile as he turned to his date. "And now I've found her."

She leaned in, allowing the curve of her breast to rub against his arm, a blatant signal that failed to pique his interest.

"Are you ready to go?" he asked.

Her smile was slow, deliberately seductive. "I've been ready for a while."

She slid a perfectly manicured hand into the crook of his elbow and tossed her hair over her shoulder. He couldn't help but contrast her polished facade to Lara's natural beauty, her neatly filed but unpainted nails, the choppy chin-length layers of her auburn hair, the subtle scent she wore.

Mi Dios. The woman was driving him crazy.

It was hell to want so desperately what he couldn't have, and crazy to be thinking about her when he was with a beautiful woman who was offering everything a man should want.

The best thing, he knew, would be to keep his distance from the nanny, to find a woman who could help him forget about Lara. But as his date edged closer, he knew that woman wouldn't be Chantal—and it wouldn't be tonight.

* * *

Lara told herself she didn't care if Rowan spent the night with Chantal St. Laurent, but it was a lie.

The thought of him with the other woman—kissing her, touching her, making love with her—was unbearable. She knew that the few kisses she'd shared with the prince didn't give her any proprietary rights, but there was nothing logical about her feelings.

She was aware that he would be getting married soon. In fact, planning for the big event was already in full swing despite the fact that he had yet to choose his bride.

Still, she couldn't help but wonder what might have developed between them if not for that wedding date looming ahead. Though she knew his impending marriage wasn't the only obstacle to a relationship. Maybe if she wasn't the nanny…or if he wasn't a prince…

She shook her head, banishing such fantasies from her mind. There was no point in wondering "what if," no hope of changing the circumstances. She might not like the idea of him marrying Chantal St. Laurent, but the reality was that he was going to get married. And if Lara was going to stay on as the royal nanny after his marriage, she was going to have to respect whomever he chose as his bride.

In the meantime, it would probably be best if she kept her distance from him. Kisses like the one they'd shared in the library today weren't just inappropriate, they were dangerous, because every time she was with him, she fell a little bit more in love.

When she got back to the palace, she went up to the nursery to peek in on the children. Damon was sleeping soundly, though the covers that were twisted around his body suggested he'd tossed and turned for a while. She carefully untangled the sheets and blankets and tucked them back up around him. Lexi was on top of her quilt with her favorite teddy bear hugged tightly against her chest. Lara lifted the little girl up to pull back the blankets, then she slid her into bed between the sheets.

As she closed the door behind her, Chantal's words echoed in her mind. *And as soon as he and I are married, you'll be gone.*

She really hoped Rowan wouldn't choose Chantal as his bride. While there was no doubt they made a beautiful couple, she wanted to believe the prince was looking for a wife whose IQ was at least higher than her enhanced bust size.

She shook off the words and the worry as she moved on to Christian's room. There was a sliver of light from beneath the door, so she tapped lightly on it before entering.

He was propped up in his bed, an open book balanced on his bent knees.

"Just a little longer?" Christian asked hopefully.

It was next to impossible for her to refuse him anything when he looked at her with those deep brown eyes that were so like his uncle's. But not completely impossible. "You've already had a lot longer than usual."

"But I'm just getting to the good part."

"The words won't fade from the pages if you leave it until tomorrow."

He rolled his eyes as he closed the book.

She glanced at the cover as she took it from him. Victor Hugo's *Hunchback of Nôtre Dame.* "That's pretty heavy bedtime reading. Are you enjoying it?"

"It was one of my dad's favorites."

Which said so much without actually answering her question. "Is that why you're reading it?"

"He always said that literature was the key to understanding so many things."

She nodded. "He loved to read. Just as Rowan loves music, Eric loves the sea and Marcus loves his horses. And you—" she said, taking the book from his hand and setting it on the bedside table "—need to find what you love."

"I'm going to be a man that my father would be proud of," Christian told her.

"Yes, you will," she agreed. "No matter what your interests or hobbies."

His brow furrowed at that, but he made no further protest when she reached to switch off the light beside his bed.

As she leaned over to touch her lips to her forehead, he squirmed just a little beneath his covers. It wouldn't be very much longer before he balked at being tucked in by the nanny, but for now he still tolerated the gesture.

"Good night, my charming prince."

He smiled at that as he fought back a yawn. "Good night."

She was yawning, too, as she made her way down the hall, though she knew she wouldn't be able to sleep just yet.

It was almost midnight, and she could see from her bedroom window that Rowan's office was dark. He was with Chantal. She had to accept that. There was no point in waiting for him to come home when she didn't even know if he would do so, no point in torturing herself with thoughts of what he was doing.

She'd denied her growing feelings for a long time, but she could deny them no longer. Somehow she'd fallen in love with the prince, and now her heart would end up broken. She only wished she could have experienced the pleasure of making love with him before losing him forever.

The tap on her door was so quiet she was sure she'd imagined it.

Then it came again, a little louder, and her pulse skipped.

She smoothed her hands down the front of her dress as she crossed the room, as hope beat frantically inside her heart. Then she opened the door, and he was there.

"I saw your light on."

That was all he said. It wasn't the words that made her throat dry and her knees weak, but the same naked desire she'd seen in his eyes when he'd kissed her in the library. And she knew that this was her chance—if she had the courage to take it—to have what her heart most wanted, at least for this one night.

Her fingers were still clamped around the knob as she tried to keep her tone steady. "Should I tell you that I couldn't sleep? Or should I tell you that I was waiting for you?"

His eyes darkened. "Were you?"

She nodded. "Are you going to come in?"

"Do you understand what will happen if I walk through that door?"

"Yes." Her voice didn't falter, her gaze didn't waver.

"You need to be sure, Lara." His eyes bored into hers and heat radiated from his body, taut with tension. "Because once I cross that threshold, there will be no going back."

She stepped away from the door so he could enter.

Chapter Ten

The door closed behind Rowan with a soft click, but he made no move toward her.

Could he hear the frantic pounding of her heart? Did he think she was afraid? Was he, despite his warning, giving her one last chance to change her mind? Did he honestly think either of them could turn back now?

She pushed these questions from her mind and went to him, moving into his arms and touching her lips to his. He kissed her back, his mouth hot and hungry, devastating hers with practiced skill and masterful intensity. Her lips parted on a sigh of pure pleasure, and his tongue dipped between them.

He'd kissed her before, but somehow this was different, as if they both knew that this time there would be no interruptions, no retreat. She shivered at the thought, her body humming with anticipation, her blood churning with desire.

But while she was thinking about getting naked and horizontal, he seemed content to keep on kissing her. And he continued to do so until he'd wiped every last coherent thought from her mind and it was filled with nothing but him, until she wanted nothing but Rowan.

She reached for the zipper at her back, but he gently caught her hands, drew them away.

"Let me. I've been thinking about getting you out of this dress since I first saw you in it."

Her hands fell back down at her sides. "You're sure taking your time about it."

He chuckled softly. "I don't plan on rushing anything tonight."

But he did—*finally*—unzip her, then parted the fabric to slide his hands along her skin.

"I want to savor every moment."

His lips skimmed down her throat, his tongue flicking over the fluttery pulse beating there.

"All…"

He pushed the straps over her shoulders.

"…night…"

And the silk whispered as it slid down her body to pool at her feet.

"…long."

He lifted his head, his eyes skimming over her bra and panties, his lips curving in appreciation of the pale peach-colored lace. Then he took her hand and guided her over to the bed.

Her heart pounded. Her knees trembled. Her stomach was a tangle of nerves. But far stronger than her trepidation about making love for the first time was the anticipation of making love with Rowan.

She wasn't fanciful enough to believe in love at first

sight, but she was honest enough to acknowledge there had been something between them from the very beginning. Her feelings for the prince might have begun as an innocent infatuation, but they had changed over the years, deepening and sharpening to this desperate, edgy need that pulsed inside her now.

He traced a finger along the lacy edge of her bra, a featherlight caress that skimmed over the curve of one breast, dipped into the shallow valley between them and followed the next curve up again. She just stood there, biting her lip, as tiny electric shocks danced in her veins. Then he traced the same route again with his mouth. And the delicate, moist flicks of his tongue nearly drove her wild.

Her breasts felt heavy, achy, and her nipples strained against the lace, practically begging for his touch. Finally he unfastened the clasp at the front of her bra and let it fall to the ground. She felt the heat and the hunger in his stare, but still he didn't touch her, not the way she so desperately wanted him to touch her.

Instead he shifted his gaze and hooked his fingers in the edge of her panties. Slowly…very slowly…he eased the scrap of lace over her hips…down her thighs…and to the ground.

The sensations swirling through her body clouded her mind so that rational thought was almost impossible. Still, she became aware of the fact that she was completely naked and he was still fully dressed. But when she reached for him, he caught her wrists in his hands again and shook his head.

"If I get naked with you right now, this will be over almost before it begins."

"I don't care," she said. "I want you. Now."

His lips curved in a smile that was both smug and full of promise.

"Let's do it my way this time." He nudged her onto the mattress. "I promise you won't regret it."

She decided to take him at his word. After all, he was the one with the experience—and the immensely talented and exceptionally creative hands.

Those hands skimmed over her now, making a leisurely and thorough exploration of her dips and curves. From her ankles to her knees to her thighs, heating her flesh everywhere that they touched, until she was burning with a desire she'd never imagined.

She shivered when his tongue swirled around one nipple, and gasped when his teeth closed gently around the taut peak and fiery spears of pleasure rocketed through her body.

As his lips and tongue and teeth continued their exquisite torment of her breasts, he slid a knee between hers, nudging apart her thighs. He parted the moist folds of swollen flesh and eased a finger into her. She sucked in a startled breath, then released it on a moan when he slowly withdrew. In and out. Slowly. Deeply. When she'd grown accustomed to that, he inserted two fingers. Slowly. Deeply. In and out. Until she felt everything inside her tense, then shatter.

Her body was still trembling with the aftershocks when he finally stripped away his clothes. She blinked to clear the haze from her eyes, and sighed happily at the sight of the fabulously sculpted and gloriously naked male body. Then sighed again as her palms slid over the hard planes of his chest, the strong curve of his shoulders and the solid muscles of his back.

He took a moment to sheath himself with a condom, then rose over her. The gentle exploration of his fingers had guaranteed she was ready for the act, but nothing could have prepared her for his size. The tip of his erection nudged against her, and she instinctively tensed, waiting for the painful thrust.

Instead, he kissed her again.

The masterful seduction of his lips swept away all of her fears and apprehensions on a misty fog of desire. Only when her body had completely relaxed and her heart had completely surrendered did he ease into her.

There was a brief moment of pain when he pushed through the barrier of her virginity, and she bit down on her lip to keep from crying out. But she must have made some kind of sound, because Rowan immediately froze. And when she arched up, wanting to take him completely, he growled at her, "Hold still a minute."

She could tell that *he* was trying to do just that, and that the effort was costing him. His jaw was clenched tight and the muscles in his arms quivered from the strain of holding himself immobile above her. Though she appreciated his consideration, she wanted his passion. She wanted to know that the fiery desire that raged through her body also raged through his.

"I don't want to hold still." She pulled his head down to kiss him again, then whispered against his lips, "I want you. All the way inside of me." She let her hips gyrate slowly. "I want to feel…everything."

"You're killing me." But he gave in to her request—or maybe his own need—and let himself sink into her.

Deep.

Deeper.

Then he began to move, long slow strokes gradually quickening, leading her from the edge of contented bliss toward the pinnacle of a greater unknown pleasure.

It was so much more than she'd anticipated, more than

she'd even hoped. New and exciting sensations bombarded her with every touch of his hands, every brush of his lips, every shift of his body. She gloried in his weight pressing down on her, the delicious friction of his damp flesh sliding over hers, the rapid beat of his heart against hers.

She rose up, locked her legs around him, and snapped the last of his restraint. His mouth crushed down on hers. Their tongues tangled, their bodies fused. This was no longer a civilized seduction but a frantic primal mating.

Her fingers dug into his shoulders; her nails raked down his back. He nipped at her earlobe; scraped his teeth over her jaw. Desires warred. Needs clashed. Wants clamored. Until the battle pushed them both over the edge and into the abyss of ultimate pleasure.

They made love again and again through the night, until their mutual exhaustion finally overwhelmed their seemingly insatiable need for each other, and they fell asleep, their bodies still tangled together.

Rowan didn't know how long they slept, and though the sky was still dark when he awoke, he knew it wouldn't be for very much longer. He had to get back to his own apartment, to shower and prepare for his day. But he let himself linger a minute longer, watching Lara sleep, wanting what he had no right to want.

And knowing he was damned.

There was no doubt in his mind about that. He'd taken her selfishly, for his own pleasure, knowing that he would marry someone else. That she understood his obligation to do so was no excuse for what he'd done.

He would burn in the fires of hell for that, but right now, with her warm and naked body snuggled close to his own, he felt as if he'd glimpsed a little piece of heaven.

Even knowing that he'd broken so many unwritten rules, he couldn't help wanting her again.

He stroked a hand over her gently, marveling at the creamy perfection and warm softness of her skin. She stirred in response to the caress, then snuggled closer to him. His body responded naturally, and it took every ounce of willpower he had—and obviously more than he'd possessed last night—to ease away from her.

After he'd dressed, he went back to her bed and brushed a gentle kiss on her brow.

Her eyelids flickered, then slowly parted to reveal those stunning moss-green eyes still misty with dreams.

"I have to go," he said softly.

She pushed herself up and, when she realized the covers hadn't moved with her, tugged the sheet up to cover her naked breasts.

He didn't try to prevent the smile that curved his lips. "*Querida*, there isn't even a tiny freckle anywhere on your body that I didn't see or touch or taste last night."

Her cheeks flushed. "I'm a little new to this morning-after routine."

"I wish I could stay to help familiarize you with it." He brushed his lips over hers. Once. Twice.

She sighed dreamily, and the sweetness of the sound made him ache.

"You have no idea how much I wish I could stay."

"I know you can't." She slid out of bed, allowing him a brief glimpse of creamy skin and tempting curves before she shoved her arms into her robe and belted it at her waist. She hesitated a moment before turning back to him. "Can I say something before you go?"

"Of course."

She took his hands. He noticed that hers trembled, just

a little, before they linked with his. "I just want you to know that last night was incredible. You showed me things I'd never even dreamed about, and I'll always be grateful for that." She looked up at him, and though her lips curved, there was a hint of sadness—or maybe it was resignation—behind the smile. "But I also knew the minute I saw you standing outside my door that whatever we shared together couldn't be anything more than a stolen moment in time. I don't expect anything more than that."

She was giving him permission to walk away without guilt or recriminations, and Rowan knew he should be grateful for that. But he wasn't grateful—he was frustrated and angry and resentful of the circumstances that demanded he walk away from the woman who had somehow taken hold of his heart.

He squeezed her hands gently. "I wish I could give you more."

And that, not just the words but the raw honesty in his voice, was what made him a prince even more than the fact that he'd been born royal—and only one of the reasons Lara loved him. But she didn't tell him that. She wouldn't burden him with the feelings that were her own. She didn't want any regrets or remorse to mar the beauty of what they had shared.

"You have a country to run and a wedding to plan," she said lightly, hoping her forced cheer concealed the heaviness in her heart.

"I wish—"

Quickly—almost desperately—she rose up on her toes and pressed her lips to his. Whatever he wanted to say, she didn't want to hear it. Because she understood only too well about wishes—and that wishing couldn't make dreams come true. "You have to go now."

He nodded. But he kissed her again before he left— softly, deeply, thoroughly.

She didn't try to go back to sleep after he'd gone. Instead, she watched the darkness of night give way to the light of day and tried not to yearn for what she couldn't have.

Elena Leandres scowled at the young woman seated in her parlor, a cup of her favorite imported coffee already in her hand. The princess drew in a deep breath and reminded herself that though the other woman was a business associate of sorts, she was also a commoner and possibly unfamiliar with protocol. She wasn't entirely convinced it was true but found it easier to tolerate ignorance than insolence. In any event, until Elena knew that the task had been completed, she could tolerate a fair amount.

She settled herself into her favorite wing chair and accepted the cup of fragrant Jamaican Blue Mountain roast a servant handed to her.

She took a long sip of her coffee, savoring the flavor, before turning to her guest. "I wasn't expecting a report at seven o'clock in the morning," Elena told her. "Did the prince regent have an early meeting today?"

"I wouldn't know," Chantal said flatly.

Elena set her cup back in the saucer. "What do you mean?"

"I mean nothing happened. The prince accompanied me home at the end of our date, saw me up to my apartment, then gave me a very chaste kiss on the cheek and walked away."

"That wasn't our plan."

Chantal tossed her hair over her shoulder. "Believe me, I wasn't too happy about the way the night ended, either."

"Obviously you didn't try hard enough."

"I could have had any man in that room."

"And yet the prince somehow managed to resist your irresistible charms?"

"It seemed that his attention was focused a little closer to home."

"It's too early for riddles," Elena snapped. "If you have something to say, say it."

But Chantal took another sip from her cup before doing so. "I got the impression he has something going with one of his staff," she finally said. "Some wide-eyed Irish girl, all sweetness and innocence."

Elena's mind was already racing ahead, considering the possibilities, but she remained cautious. "Are you sure about this?"

"I didn't actually see them going at it," Chantal said drily. "But there were some pretty serious vibes passing between them."

"Do you know who she is? What her name is?"

"Lana or Laura. Something like that." She gave a dismissive shrug. "I don't remember, but I know she's the nanny."

The prince regent was sleeping with the nanny of his brother's children?

Elena smiled. This might work out even better than her original plan.

August thirtieth was the date that had been set for the royal wedding. A little more than four months away, and Henri liked to remind Rowan of the deadline every morning, hoping it would encourage the prince regent to focus his attention on finding a bride. Instead, Rowan was haunted by memories of the night he'd spent in Lara's bed—of her soft lips yielding to his, her naked body moving beneath his, her heart beating in rhythm with his.

He'd thought it would be enough to have her once, that

the experience would satisfy his craving for her and his infatuation would fade. Instead, he only wanted her more.

He'd wanted to believe it was the forbidden nature of the attraction that made her so hard to resist. But in the darkness of night, in the warmth of her arms, he'd realized it was—and had always been—Lara. She was so sweet and loving and giving, and somehow, she'd completely taken hold of his heart.

It was that realization that worried him more than the illicitness of their relationship that made him determined to stay away. But when he finally left his office shortly after midnight, he found himself detouring past her rooms on the way to his own.

She let him in, no questions asked, and moved willingly into his arms. She was inexperienced but uninhibited, and Rowan realized that nothing he'd ever experienced was more arousing than a woman discovering the pleasures of sex. Nothing was more satisfying than making love to a woman who tempted him to fall in love again.

He had her out of her nightgown before they moved away from the door, then discarded his own clothes on the way to her bed.

He'd once thought she was like Margot, and he'd resented her for that. He'd resented the fact that he only had to look at her and he wanted.

Margot had been attracted to him because of his royal status, and she'd used his desire for her to manipulate him. She'd twisted his feelings for her own purposes, lied to him and deceived him, until there was nothing left in his heart but contempt. Her fraudulent claim that she was carrying his child was the final straw, and when Rowan had walked away from her the last time, he'd been certain he would never open up his heart again.

And he'd never even been tempted to do so.

Until Lara.

He knew now that Lara wasn't anything like Margot. She seemed to want him almost in spite of his title. And she'd given him more than anyone else ever had, more than he'd had any right to take. With her he could forget everything else and just be. She didn't seem to want anything *from* him, she only wanted him, and that was a new and novel experience for a man who had been born a prince.

She drew him down onto the bed with her, and their bodies merged and moved together as if they'd been joined this way a thousand times before. If he let himself think about it, he might wonder about the fact that no one had made him feel this way before, and he might worry that he would never want—could never want—anyone but Lara again.

But there was no room for such disquieting thoughts now. In this moment there was only Lara. She filled his mind, his heart, his soul.

As he emptied himself into her, he realized that she had given him everything, and he wondered how he would ever be able to settle for anything less.

Lara hadn't expected that Rowan would come to her again. He'd taken a risk, spending most of the previous night in her room, and though she had absolutely no regrets, she wasn't sure that he didn't. Because he was a prince and required to abide by a whole different set of standards and rules, and sleeping with the nanny was against all of them.

Now they'd broken those rules again, but she didn't care. Nothing mattered but being in his arms and knowing she was wanted by this incredible man. *The prince might take you to his bed, but he'll never take you as his wife.*

She shook off the memory of Chantal's scathing remark. She didn't need to remember the words to know her relationship with Rowan wouldn't last forever. For Lara, for now, being with him was enough.

"I didn't think you would come tonight," she admitted, as she cuddled close to him in her bed.

"I shouldn't have."

She wasn't bothered by his response. How could she be when his fingers were gliding over her skin, tracing a path from her shoulder to her hip, sending deliciously erotic tingles through every part of her body?

"I'm not sorry." She snuggled closer, so that the tips of her breasts rubbed his chest, and smiled when she felt his body responding.

"I'm not sorry, either. But that doesn't change the fact that I shouldn't be here. I shouldn't be with you while I'm planning to marry someone else." His arms tightened around her. "But it's you I can't stop thinking about. You I can't stop wanting."

"I can't stop thinking about you or wanting you, either," she admitted.

And then, because she knew the issue wouldn't stop being a barrier between them no matter how much she wanted to ignore it, she said, "I understand you told the children that you're getting married."

"I thought they should know."

"Of course," she agreed. "But you should know that Lexi has her heart set on being a flower girl. Then, when she explained the role to Damon, he insisted that he should be a flower girl, too, but I think she's almost convinced him that ring bearer is a more appropriate role for him."

"Apparently she knows more about getting married than I do."

"A lot of little girls have a fascination with weddings, maybe because so many fairy tales have a wedding before the happily ever after."

"It didn't occur to me to include the children."

"You might want to consider it," she said, "since your wife will be a strong presence in their lives."

She tried to keep her voice light, but it was awkward to talk about him marrying another woman while she was naked in his arms.

Rowan apparently didn't want to talk about his wedding, either, because he asked, "Did your mother read fairy tales to you when you were a little girl?"

"No. She was afraid they would give me ideas, and she wanted me to know that there was no prince out there who would ride into my life on a white horse and carry me off to live in his castle in the sky.

"But when I was about nine years old, I got a book of fairy tales out of the library at school. I was immediately captivated by the story of Rapunzel. Not that my mother ever locked me in a tower or even a closet, but I felt trapped in my life. I knew my mother didn't want me, and it was my greatest fantasy to someday find someone who did.

"I read that story over and over again," she admitted. "And afterward I refused to get my hair cut. Despite my mother's warnings, I was young enough and silly enough to believe that if I could grow my hair as long as Rapunzel's, my prince would come."

He sifted his fingers through her short, silky hair. "Then someone broke your heart and you got it chopped off."

"Nothing so melodramatic," she assured him. "I simply grew up and realized it was ridiculous to pin my hopes on someone else rescuing me from the mediocrity of my life.

If I wanted things to change, I would have to make the effort to change them myself."

"And your dreams?"

"Are different now."

"Do you ever wonder about your father?" he asked. "Who he is, where he might be?"

"I used to, but after my mom died, I realized that the possibility of finding him was just another fairy tale."

"What about a family of your own? You must want to get married someday, have children."

It was what she wanted more than anything in the world—someone to love and who would love her in return, a family of her own, a place where she truly belonged. But there was no point in sharing those dreams with a man who could never be the prince of her dreams.

"Someday," she agreed, then smiled. "But *I'm* still young enough not to have to worry about things like that right now."

He scowled at her, proving that her playful taunt had succeeded in diverting his attention.

"I might have ten years on you," he acknowledged. "But I can handle anything you can dream up."

"Anything?" She leaned closer, whispered a very explicit suggestion in his ear. "You think you're up to that challenge?"

He responded by flipping her onto her back, trapping her beneath his very hard, very aroused body, and proceeded to prove that he was up for anything.

And they both forgot about weddings and fairy tales and everything else but the pleasure of each other.

Chapter Eleven

Marcus was home for the summer.

Under normal circumstances, Rowan would have been pleased by his brother's return, not just because he could shift some of his responsibilities—at least temporarily—onto Marcus's very capable shoulders, but because he enjoyed his company. But nothing had been "normal" since Julian and Catherine had died, and Rowan wasn't sure how long he could continue sneaking into Lara's room in the night without his brother beginning to suspect just how much his relationship with the nanny had changed in the few months that Marcus had been gone.

It was an entirely different matter that was on his brother's mind, however, when he came to Rowan's office Thursday morning.

"What's going on in the ballroom?" Marcus asked. "It

looks like a strategic planning session of the war department."

"You've been in America too long," Rowan told his brother. "We don't have a war department."

"Tell that to the two women who were battling over lilies and orchids. I thought there was going to be bloodshed."

"Ah, yes. They would be the frontline soldiers in our new matrimonial regiment."

"Do I want to know?"

"Henri hired a wedding planner. The wedding planner decided he needed a veritable army of assistants to see to all the intricate details of the royal wedding."

"Including the finding of a bride?"

"No, apparently that's still my responsibility. Unless, of course, you're here to tell me that the legislation is invalid and I'm not actually required to get married at the end of August."

Marcus shook his head. "Not yet, but I'm looking into some things."

"Don't rush into anything," Rowan said drily.

"Well, I wouldn't want to get you off the hook too soon and deprive you of the company of all the beautiful and willing women who hope to be chosen as your bride."

"I'm glad you find this amusing, because I'm just finding it tiresome."

"Sometimes I can't believe you're my brother," Marcus lamented.

"Look at this." Rowan opened his drawer and pulled out a paper. "This is a list of potential bridal candidates and the 'dates' that have been set up for the next several weeks."

Marcus skimmed the list of names. "Alphabetical order?"

Rowan shrugged. "Henri thought it was the most impartial method of organizing the candidates."

"Henri put this together for you?"

"He volunteered to help sort through the mail. You wouldn't believe how many letters and pictures have flooded in since the media announced that I was looking for a bride."

"Imagine how many disappointed women there would be if they ever found out you're just going through the motions." Marcus tapped a finger against one of the names on the list. "Ava Medeiros…?"

"You know her?"

His brother's only response was a slow grin. "Yeah, and while I don't doubt you would enjoy her…company, I'm not sure you should consider her a candidate for marriage."

Rowan handed him a pen. "Cross her off the list—along with anyone else who might be uncomfortable seated across from you at the dinner table."

"I assure you, they all have fond memories of me, which would only make things awkward for *you*."

"I appreciate your consideration." He noticed that his brother had struck three other names from the list, including Chantal St. Laurent. "So much for thinking your reputation was exaggerated."

Marcus's grin returned. "I assure you it was earned through a most dedicated effort."

"If only you would apply that single-minded focus to some other pursuit."

"I can't imagine anything else so immensely pleasurable."

"That's the real reason you chose to go to university in America, isn't it? Because you'd dated most of the women in Europe."

"That might have been a factor," his brother allowed. "But Harvard does have a pretty good reputation as a law school. And it turns out that I'm actually learning some stuff. In fact, I finished third in my class this year."

Rowan glanced up. "And you tell me this as if it's an afterthought?"

"It's not really a big deal."

"Of course it is." He felt a twinge of guilt for riding his brother so hard about his reputation. The truth was, he'd often envied Marcus's charm and easygoing nature that led to his success, not just with women but with anything he put his mind to. "And I'm proud of you."

Marcus shrugged, but Rowan could tell he was pleased—if a little embarrassed—by the praise.

"Do you have any plans to celebrate the end of term—or did you do enough celebrating in Boston?"

"I didn't do anything that made headlines," Marcus said. "Then again, in America, we're considered minor royalty and not worthy of much attention."

"Are you planning to make headlines here?"

"Nope—just looking forward to a night on the town with a beautiful woman."

"I should have guessed," he said, then had to ask, "Is her name on the list?"

"No."

Even in that monosyllabic response, there was something that alerted Rowan. "Anyone I know?"

"I'm going out with Lara tonight."

"You're joking."

Marcus raised his brows. "Why is that so unbelievable?"

"Because…" He didn't know how to answer the question in a way that wouldn't lead his brother into asking more, so all he said was, "She's not even your type."

"I try not to limit myself to any particular type—there are too many unique and interesting women out there."

"But Lara is…Lara."

Marcus's eyes narrowed. "It seems your opinion of her has changed over the past couple of months."

"I've come to appreciate her importance to the household through her relationship with the children," Rowan remarked carefully.

"Hmm," was his brother's only response.

"Which is why I don't think it's a good idea for you to go out with her."

"It's just dinner and a movie, and we'll be well chaperoned."

"Chaperoned?"

Now his brother grinned. "Christian, Lexi and Damon are coming with us."

The wave of relief brought on by this revelation was as irrational as the surge of jealousy that had hit when Marcus mentioned Lara's name, especially considering that he'd been working his way through Henri's list despite spending most of his nights in her bed.

"I'm glad the children are going, too," Rowan said. "They really enjoy spending time with you."

"That's because I'm immature and not afraid to make a fool of myself."

"You underestimate yourself," he said, and realized that he had done so, as well. His brother wasn't a reckless teenager anymore but an adult—maybe not entirely grown-up yet but well on his way.

"What are your plans for tonight?" Marcus asked. "Because you're welcome to join us, if you like."

"I wish I could. But I'm attending a dinner party with—" he glanced at the list "—number fourteen tonight."

"You should keep an open mind. Number fourteen could be your wife in a few short months."

"Thanks for the reminder," he said drily.

Marcus grinned again. "Glad to help."

When Lara showed up at Tanis's apartment the following afternoon, she found her usually unruffled friend was decidedly ruffled. The cause of her stress became apparent when Tanis dumped a pile of bridal magazines at Lara's feet and said, "Help."

Lara picked one off the top and began to thumb through it. "What is it, exactly, that you need my help with?"

"Everything. Dresses, flowers, cake. My mind is spinning with all of the details."

"You were the one who wanted a fall wedding."

"I know." She dropped onto Lara's sofa. "Can I borrow your wedding planner?"

"He's Rowan's wedding planner, not mine."

Tanis winced. "I'm sorry. That was incredibly tactless of me."

"I'm well aware of the fact that he's getting married," Lara said. "You don't need to tiptoe around the subject."

Her friend sighed. "I just wish you'd found someone else to fall in love with so we could be planning our weddings together."

"We can still have fun planning yours."

"You're not denying that you're in love with him," Tanis noted.

She shrugged. "You'd know I was lying if I even tried."

"You slept with him, didn't you?"

She couldn't prevent the smile that curved her lips. "Yeah."

"I'm guessing he wasn't a big disappointment?"

"No."

Tanis sighed. "I was afraid of that."

Lara reached over to squeeze her friend's hands. "Please don't worry about me. I went into this with my eyes wide open."

"How can I not worry? You're in love with a prince."

"No," Lara said. "I'm in love with a man who happens to be a prince." And if she'd learned nothing else over the past few months, she'd learned that Rowan was so much more than his title, so much more than anyone else she'd ever known.

"I knew it was a bad idea for you to go back there."

"I don't regret my decision."

"And when the prince marries someone else?"

"I've known from the beginning that our relationship could only be temporary."

"And that's enough for you?" Tanis demanded.

"It's more than I've ever had before—more than I ever thought I would."

"And when it's over, you're going to be left with less than nothing because there's no way you'll be able to continue working there, seeing him day after day, hovering on the periphery while he builds a life with his new bride."

It was a reality she knew she'd have to face soon enough but one that she refused to think about until then. So she forced a smile and asked, "Did you want to talk about the prince regent's wedding or your own?"

Tan narrowed her eyes. "You're trying to change the subject."

"Only because I want to make sure I won't have to wear cotton-candy pink ruffles."

"No pink," her friend promised. "And definitely no ruffles."

* * *

Rowan knew Lara was gone even before he reached for her and found the bed empty. Or maybe it was the sudden awareness of her absence that had awakened him.

He gathered up his clothes and dressed in the dark, puzzling over the fact that he could wake up missing her just because she wasn't there beside him. Definitely not a good sign.

He tripped on a pile of magazines beside the sofa.

Tanis's bridal magazines, Lara had hastened to assure him when he'd spotted one on her night table. Then she'd told him about her friend's engagement to the gallery owner and explained that Tanis wanted help in picking out a gown.

Rowan had found himself wondering when Lara would get to pick out her own wedding dress, thinking about the kind of man she would choose to marry and wishing it could be him. He realized that wanting what he knew was an impossible dream was just another sign that he was in way too deep.

He checked the hall before he stepped out of her room. Not that he expected anyone else to be wandering the corridors at this hour, but he couldn't chance it. He wasn't ashamed of his relationship with Lara, but he was worried about her reputation. Not enough to stay away, obviously, but enough to not want her to be hurt by their affair. Except that, in his heart, he knew it was already too late to protect her—or himself.

But instead of heading up to his own apartment, as he'd intended to do, he went across the hall to Damon's room and found her there. No doubt she'd been summoned from her bed by one of his young nephew's nightmares, though he hadn't heard a sound. The child was sleeping peacefully now, as Lara was, too, curled up in a chair that she'd pulled close to the side of Damon's bed.

It never ceased to impress him how easily she anticipated and responded to the needs of his brother's children. Part of that, he knew, was familiarity with them and their routines. And part, he suspected, was simply her innate compassion and nurturing spirit. The same compassion and nurturing spirit she had shown to him in so many ways, not the least of which was helping him to finally accept Julian's and Catherine's deaths and move on with his own life. And moving on for Rowan meant choosing a bride.

Though the law required that he marry a woman of certain qualifications, his heart warned that he would find no other woman who mattered as much as this one who was so unsuitable simply because of the location and circumstances of her birth. He was hardly the first ruler to face this conflict between duty and desire—and he knew it wasn't a conflict he could continue to ignore.

With that thought in mind, he lifted her from the chair and into his arms. She stirred but didn't awaken, a sign of how truly exhausted she was. He carried her back to her own room and laid her gently on the bed.

"Rowan?"

He pulled up the covers, then brushed his lips against hers gently. "Go back to sleep."

"Where are you going?" she murmured the question, still more asleep than awake.

"Upstairs," he said. "I have early meetings this morning."

"Is it morning already?"

"Not quite."

Her eyes drifted closed again. "Stay."

He wished he could—not just for another hour or

another night, but for always. But he suspected that even if he could have forever with her, it wouldn't be enough. And forever was impossible, anyway. Even these past few weeks had been nothing more than a dream and it was time—for both their sakes—to stop living in a fantasy and start living up to his responsibilities.

It was time to let her go.

Lara glanced from the clock to the window. It was 2:00 a.m. and the light was still on in Rowan's office. Obviously he wasn't going to come to her tonight.

Though less than five weeks had passed since the first night they'd made love, he'd been with her more often than not during that time. And on the occasions that he did have to work late or was unavailable because of other duties, he'd made a point of letting her know in advance—and telling her that he'd be thinking of her.

But she hadn't seen or heard from him at all in three days, and now she couldn't help but wonder if there was some kind of crisis that was keeping him away—or if he'd simply grown bored with her.

She'd known from the beginning that their relationship couldn't last. He was the prince regent, after all, and she was illegitimate and untitled and an employee of the royal household. Yes, she'd accepted that there was no future for them together, but her heart wasn't ready to give him up just yet. She wouldn't accept that it was over until she heard those words from Rowan.

The knots in her belly tightened with every step she took as she made her way through the maze of corridors to his office.

She heard the music first. He'd introduced her to the works of several classical composers, and she recognized the piece playing in the background as one of Bach's violin concertos. Then she saw him.

He was seated at his desk, but his chair had been turned to the side and his gaze was focused somewhere outside the window. Her heart sank further as her suspicions were confirmed—the only work Rowan was doing in here tonight was avoiding her.

She was tempted to go, to leave before he knew she was there. Though her heart wanted to run and hide, her pride wouldn't let her be so easily dismissed.

"Were you afraid that I'd make a scene?" She was pleased that her voice was calm, giving no indication of the emotions that were churning her up inside. "Or am I so insignificant that I don't deserve the courtesy of a personal breakup?"

Something flashed across his face—guilt? Regret? Yearning? Whatever it was, it was quickly masked and she found herself confronting the impenetrable facade of the prince regent.

"You were never insignificant," he told her.

Her throat was tight. "Wasn't I?"

A muscle flexed in his jaw. "It had to end sometime—we both knew that."

Yes, they had both known it. But that didn't make the reality of it any easier. And after everything they'd shared—the passion, the camaraderie, the laughter—this distant politeness was unbearable.

"I guess my mistake was in thinking we would *both* decide when 'sometime' came."

"I never made you any promises," he reminded her.

"I never asked for any."

"No, you didn't," he acknowledged. "But the people of

Tesoro del Mar do have certain expectations, and I need to fulfill them."

She wanted to say it before he did—before he shattered her heart with the words. "You've chosen a bride."

"I've invited Lady Victoria Barrow to come to the palace for dinner Friday night to meet the children."

It wasn't precisely a confirmation, but she knew that meeting the children was a necessary formality before he asked Victoria to marry him. Not certain she could trust her voice, she merely nodded in response to his announcement.

He stood now and came around his desk, but didn't move any closer to her. She told herself she was glad for that. If he touched her, if he showed the slightest hint of compassion, she would fall apart, and she didn't want to do that. At least not until she was alone.

"I was going to tell you," he said. "I didn't want you to hear about it from anyone else."

She'd honestly believed she could accept the inevitability of his marriage to someone else, but her shattered heart proved otherwise. She'd loved him and she'd lost him, and the pain of that loss was unbearable.

She grasped at the fraying threads that were all that remained of her composure. "Well, thank you for that, anyway." She turned away from him. "I'll let you get back to your work now."

Blinded by the tears that filled her eyes, she fumbled for the knob.

"Lara—"

She heard the emotion in his voice now—both longing and regret. But she walked out, pretending she didn't hear him at all.

* * *

Rowan knew he'd made the right decision in ending his relationship with Lara. It wasn't fair to continue sharing her bed while planning his wedding to someone else. But she remained in his thoughts and in his heart.

And though he'd decided that Lady Victoria Barrow was the most suitable choice for his bride, he knew he would never love her as much as he loved Lara.

It didn't matter, of course. He wasn't expected to marry for love, but only as a means of securing his position and his nephew's entitlement to the throne. Thankfully, Victoria didn't seem to expect any declaration of affection. She was an eminently practical woman, which was one of the reasons he'd decided she'd be an appropriate wife for him.

He didn't want a woman who expected more than he could give, and he couldn't give any woman his heart.

That belonged to Lara.

It had been his intention to propose to Victoria after dinner with the children Friday night. He hadn't bought a ring because he didn't know her well enough to guess what she would like, but he figured she could pick out whatever she wanted after their engagement was official.

Dinner had gone smoothly enough and as they'd lingered over dessert and coffee after the children had been dismissed, he'd learned a fair bit about the British woman—her family background, her education, her goals for the future. But every time he'd thought of asking her to marry him, he'd felt something like panic rising into his throat rather than the words he needed to say.

It was as if the more time he spent with her, the more he realized she was exactly the kind of woman he *should* want to marry, but she wasn't at all the woman he wanted.

He was still pondering his indecision Saturday morning when his nephew walked into his office.

"Are you going to marry Lady Victoria Barrow?" Christian asked without preamble.

He should have answered the question with an assertive and enthusiastic "yes." Instead, he heard himself respond, "I haven't made any final decision."

"But you don't love her."

He frowned, wondering how his nephew could be so certain of that fact but unable to deny it himself. "There are a lot of factors a man must consider before deciding to marry—love is only one of them."

"Isn't it the most important one?"

Rowan didn't know how to begin to explain the conflict between duty and desire, but he also couldn't ignore the issue when it was a dilemma his nephew might also have to face some day. "Yes," he finally said. "Love is—or should be for most people—the primary consideration for marrying. But a political figure or national leader—like us—must consider other factors, as well, such as a potential bride's suitability for the responsibilities she will need to fulfill."

"My dad loved my mom."

Rowan heard the question within the statement and felt the familiar pang for everything that had been lost when Julian and Catherine died, but he nodded. "Yes, he did. He loved your mom more than anything else, except maybe you and your brother and sister."

"He would have wanted the same thing for you."

"He also knew that a prince sometimes has to put the needs of his country ahead of his own."

"Okay—so you have to get married," Christian acknowledged. "But you don't have to marry Lady Victoria Barrow."

"You seemed to get on well enough with Lady Victoria at dinner," he noted.

Christian's gaze dropped. "She seemed nice enough at dinner."

"What happened to change your opinion?"

"I overheard her talking to Lara," he admitted. "I didn't mean to eavesdrop, but then I heard her mention us—me and Lexi and Damon."

Rowan frowned. Though he felt he should reprimand his nephew for listening to a conversation that wasn't intended for his ears, he was more curious about the content of that conversation. "What did she say?"

"She said that we were ill-mannered and undisciplined."

And Rowan had thought they'd come a long way in the past couple of months, since that first disastrous dinner shortly after Lara had returned to the palace.

"Lady Victoria doesn't have a lot of experience with children," he told his nephew. "She just needs a chance to get to know you better."

"She doesn't want to know us better. She wants to send us to military school."

"Military school," Marcus repeated, stepping into the room. "Why would you send the kid to military school?"

"I'm not sending anyone to military school," Rowan said firmly.

"That's what you say now," his nephew said, sounding resigned to his fate. "But who knows what will happen after you're married to her?"

"Who is the 'her' your uncle is planning to marry?"

"Lady Victoria Barrow." The boy's tone was filled with resignation and regret.

Rowan wanted to reassure him, but he wasn't sure how

to do so and his mind was still reeling from Christian's revelation.

"Thank you for sharing your concerns with me," he said. "But if you don't mind, I have some business to discuss with Marcus right now."

Christian opened his mouth as if there was something else he wanted to say, but then he snapped it shut again and slipped out of the room.

"Lady Victoria Barrow?" Marcus asked.

"She's attractive and well educated, and she has distant familial connections to both the British monarchy and the American president. And she never said anything to me about military school."

"She's probably waiting for the ring on her finger before she starts making demands."

"I thought she was the best choice, but now…"

"Now you need to take another look at your options."

"Apparently."

"When I saw you and Lara having coffee together in the parlor after dinner the other night, I thought—" Marcus shook his head. "Never mind. Obviously I misinterpreted the situation."

Rowan sighed as he thought fleetingly—and regretfully—of the woman who had come to mean so much to him. "No, you probably didn't."

"Then you are involved with her?"

"Not exactly."

"*That* certainly clarifies things."

"We were involved," Rowan admitted. "Now we're not."

"You didn't look at her like a man who was uninvolved."

"Thanks for the insight, king of one-night relationships."

Marcus just shrugged, not offended by the sarcasm. "I *have* dated a lot of women, which is why I can assure you there aren't many out there like Lara. You've been worrying about this impending six-month deadline, but I promise if you let her go, you'll spend the rest of your life regretting it."

"If I defy the law to be with Lara—" and the thought had been hammering at his mind, the possibility tempting his aching heart with the promise of something even greater than he could dream "—our family could lose the throne. And personally, I couldn't care less, but it's not really mine to lose. It should be Christian's when he is of age to rule, and I won't do anything to jeopardize his birthright."

Marcus tossed a folder onto his brother's desk. "There might be another option."

Chapter Twelve

Lara knew an official announcement of the prince's engagement would come from the palace's PR department, but she suspected that if Rowan had proposed to Victoria the previous night, the woman wouldn't be able to contain her excitement. She would have told someone, and that someone would have told someone else, and soon the media would be crawling all over the story.

So she was surprised that there was no mention of an impending engagement announcement in the paper, but not surprised when a call came through to her room from a man who identified himself as Alex Girard, a society reporter with *La Noticia,* the local paper. She didn't know how he'd got her number or why he thought she might be willing to share inside information, but she understood the "no comment" policy of palace officials and was prepared to use it when he asked about the prince's engagement.

She wasn't prepared for the reporter to ask about *her*.

"Is it true that you got the job as the royal nanny because of a family connection?"

The question seemed benevolent enough, so she responded, "It's true that I met Princess Catherine through a distant family connection."

"When the princess hired you to care for her children, did she know about your family history?"

"I beg your pardon?"

"Did she know that your mother was never married to your father? Or that your mother wasn't even sure of the identity of your father?"

Even after so many years she was ashamed by the fact, and she was grateful the reporter couldn't see the hot color she could feel in her cheeks. "The princess knew everything she needed to know about my family and my past."

"And what about the present?" he continued. "What can you tell me about the rumors that you are personally involved with the prince regent?"

She didn't know what to say, how to respond, so she said, "No comment," realizing too late that her failure to deny the allegation would be taken as an admission.

Alex Girard knew it, too, because she heard the smug satisfaction in his voice when he said, "Thank you for your time, Miss Brennan."

Then he hung up before she could undo the damage.

Even before Lara replaced the receiver, she knew that she had to tell Rowan about the reporter's call. He needed a chance to prepare a response to the accusations that would be splashed across the headlines. Or maybe he could contact Girard personally to talk about his engagement so that everything else would be forgotten.

She wasn't worried for herself. She'd lived without knowing who her father was for twenty-five years, but she did worry that the public would object to a bastard nanny working for the royal children and that Rowan wouldn't appreciate finding her at the center of another scandal. And she worried even more that the truth about her affair with Rowan, though over, would destroy his plans to marry Lady Victoria.

Which would be less of a concern, she realized, if he'd already proposed. If the other woman had a ring on her finger, Lara trusted that she'd be less likely to try to wiggle out of their engagement because of a relationship, however scandalous, that had ended before Rowan proposed. The revelation would still result in friction and distrust, and Lara knew she would have to leave the palace and the children to alleviate that.

She felt confident that the children would adapt to her absence more easily this time because of the bonds they'd formed with their uncle over the past few months. Christian rode with him at least twice a week now, Lexi had conquered her fear of the water and was letting him teach her to dive, and Damon just loved getting down on the carpet with him and racing his toy cars. If she had to leave, she would be a mess, but Rowan would make sure the children were okay.

She pushed the thought out of her mind, arriving at Rowan's office as he was leaving.

"I was on my way to find you," he said.

She knew he couldn't have spoken with Girard—if he had, he wouldn't be smiling. But she couldn't imagine what else would cause him to seek her out when their paths had barely crossed throughout the past week.

"I thought your engagement would be announced in the

paper today." She wasn't sure why she blurted the words out, except maybe as an excuse or an explanation for what she needed to tell him.

"Actually, that's why I wanted to talk to you. There's been a change of plans." He carried a folder in one hand, but reached out with the other, taking her hand and linking their fingers together. "Will you take a walk with me?"

It was a simple touch, and yet the skin-on-skin contact—even if it was only hand in hand—stirred up all the feelings she'd tried so hard to tamp down. She didn't want to break the contact, but she also knew she couldn't be seen holding hands with the prince regent in the hall—especially not with rumors of an affair circulating—so she tugged her own away. "You want to walk?"

"I have been known to do so on occasion," he said lightly.

"I don't doubt it, Your Highness." As he started toward the wide curving staircase, she fell into step behind him. "You've just never wanted to walk with me before."

"A definite oversight on my part." He lowered his voice as they passed a couple of servants on the stairs. "It seems we missed out on sharing too many of the everyday things."

The intimacy of both his tone and the words made her heart bump in her chest. "Where are we going?"

"To the rose garden."

It was one of her favorite spots on the grounds, and she wondered if he knew that and why he had chosen it as their destination. But she didn't dare ask. In fact, neither of them spoke again until they were in the privacy of the yard where the sun was starting to dip in the sky and the air was rich with the scent of imported flowers.

"The windows on the west side of my office overlook this spot," he told her. "I've seen you here, sometimes by yourself, sometimes with the children, and I watched you, wishing I could be with you—as we are now."

She wondered why he was telling her this, what difference his revelation could possibly make, and tried not to be distracted by his quiet words and lingering glances. She had to stay focused on what was important—the truth that could tear all of their lives apart.

"Do you know Alex Girard from *La Noticia?*" she asked him.

He frowned at her question as he took her hand again and led her over to the marble bench facing one of the fountains. "I know *of* him."

She sat, because his nearness was making her knees weak, and he sat beside her, so close that their bodies were almost touching. She stared at the water and tried again. "He called today," she said, "and—"

"I've missed you, Lara."

And she completely lost her train of thought.

She shifted away from him. "Rowan…"

"I had a meeting with Marcus this morning."

They were definitely off topic now, but she let him talk, figuring her turn would come when he was finished.

"Actually, I spoke with Christian first," he told her. "Why didn't you tell me that Lady Victoria wanted to send the children to military school?"

"Because I knew you wouldn't let her."

"Christian was less certain."

"I hope you reassured him."

"Since I've decided not to marry her, it's a nonissue."

So much for her hope that they were already engaged. "What do you mean you've decided not to marry her?"

"Maybe this will help." He opened the folder and took out a sheaf of papers, flipping through them until he found a page that had been highlighted, and passed it to her. Lara's eyes skimmed over the passage while he spoke.

"As it turns out, I don't have to choose a bride who fits the criteria set out by Parliament more than a hundred years ago." He looked up at her and smiled again. "I can marry anyone I want, even if she's not royal or Tesorian or—"

"Anyone you want," she interrupted, her gaze dropping back to the page. "So long as a majority of the votes cast in a referendum approve of your choice."

"I want to marry you, Lara."

Two weeks ago—even two days or two *hours* ago—she would have been thrilled to hear him say those words to her, to know that he wanted to be with her. But in the space of a two-minute phone call, everything had changed.

She could still hear the taunt of the reporter on the other end of the telephone, could all too easily imagine the headlines if Rowan chose the bastard nanny as his royal bride.

And when the referendum failed, so would his hopes of remaining on the throne.

She forced herself to meet his gaze and said, "But I don't want to marry you."

Rowan stared at her as her words echoed in his mind. He felt like an idiot for not even considering that she might not want the same thing he did. It had simply never occurred to him, after everything they'd been to each other, that she would reject him.

She laid her hand on his arm—as if the gentle touch might soften the devastating blow. "I'm just not ready to make that kind of commitment to anyone."

He had to unclench his jaw to speak. "Any idea when you might be ready?"

"I'm not asking you to wait."

And he didn't have the luxury of waiting—unless he could somehow use the legislation Marcus had dug up to amend the timeframe in which a ruler was required to marry. "What if I could?"

She shook her head. "I never said or did anything to give you the impression that I wanted to marry you."

It only made him angrier to realize that she was right. And yet, he couldn't believe the statement was a true reflection of her emotions.

There were so many things they hadn't spoken of while they were together, feelings they couldn't share because of the forbidden nature of their relationship. But not talking about them didn't make them any less real. At least, not for Rowan. And, he was willing to bet, not for Lara, either. "Then tell me what you did want," he demanded.

"Exactly what we had," she told him.

"Do you expect me to believe that it was just sex for you?"

She shrugged, but didn't meet his eyes. "I was a twenty-five-year-old virgin," she reminded him. "Yes, I wanted to know what all the fuss was about sex, and I was fortunate enough to be initiated into the art of lovemaking by a man who is clearly a master."

"That assessment doesn't flatter either of us."

"I care about you, Rowan. You know I do. But I never expected nor wanted anything more than an affair."

She was lying to him. He couldn't have said why he was so certain of it, only that he was. But the realization was little consolation to his wounded heart.

"Okay," he said, playing along for the moment. "You don't want to marry me. I guess that puts Lady Victoria back on my list of candidates."

He saw a flicker of something in her eyes. It wasn't

much, but it was enough to convince him that she wasn't as cool and unaffected as she wanted him to believe.

But then she looked up and forced a smile. "I was thinking that it might help to have the children out of the way while you're making the final preparations for your wedding. Maybe I could take them to Ireland when school is finished for the summer, so they can visit their grandparents."

"I think you're running away," he said. "The question is—from what?"

"I'm only trying to do my job."

"And if I refuse to let you go? You can hardly take the children out of the country without my permission."

"You have too much pride to make me stay where you know I don't want to be."

"I wouldn't count on that." He tipped her chin up, forcing her to meet his gaze. "And what does my pride matter if you've already taken my heart?"

She jerked her head to the side, but not before he caught a glimpse of the tears that shimmered in her eyes. When she turned back again, they were gone. "Don't try to manipulate me, Rowan."

"I'm not trying to manipulate you—I'm trying to understand why you're so intent on denying what's between us."

"There's nothing between us. Not anymore."

But there was more desperation than conviction in her tone, and he had one last card to play—and one he could hold on to no longer. "I love you, Lara."

She didn't respond. And though he still didn't understand why, he understood that she wanted him to believe their relationship truly was over.

He stood up. "I told you once before—when I fight, I fight to win. And I'm not going to give up on us without a fight."

* * *

Lara managed to hold back the tears until he'd gone, then she dropped her face into her hands and let them come.

"I didn't intend to eavesdrop."

She'd thought she was alone, and jolted at the sound of Marcus's voice.

He lowered himself into the seat recently vacated by his brother. "I was already in the garden when you and Rowan came out, and I couldn't help but overhear."

She wiped her cheeks with the back of her hand. "How much did you hear?"

"Enough to believe you actually meant what you said— until the tears started." He curled his arm around her shoulders and hugged her. "So do you want to tell me why you sent him away with his heart in jagged little pieces when you're obviously as much in love with him as he is with you?"

She tipped her head back against his shoulder and sighed. "You know," she said, ignoring his question, "if you hadn't given him ideas about changing the rules halfway through the game, he'd be engaged to Lady Victoria by now."

"And that would be a much better situation for all," he said drily.

"It would," she insisted, thinking of the reporter's phone call again.

"For your information, Rowan had already decided he couldn't marry Lady Victoria before I saw him this morning—probably because he realized what a mistake it would be to marry one woman while in love with another."

"When he's had a chance to think about it, he'll do what is right for his country, and that's marrying Lady Victoria or one of the other suitable women on his list."

"If he does, he'll be unhappy for the rest of his life." Marcus pointed out. "Is that what you want?"

"If he lost the Santiago family's right to the throne after four hundred years, he'd be more than unhappy—he'd be devastated," she insisted.

"So *that's* what this is all about," he murmured.

"I can't let him make that kind of sacrifice."

He smiled a little. "You don't know my brother very well if you think he'll appreciate you making that kind of decision for him."

"I know how much his heritage means to him."

"I wouldn't have suggested the referendum as an option if I didn't think it could succeed," Marcus said.

"You didn't have all the facts," she told him.

"Why don't you fill me in?"

So she told him about the phone call—Girard's questions about her paternity, his speculation about her relationship with Rowan, and her lame "no comment" response.

"When this all comes to light, Rowan will understand that I did the right thing, and he'll be grateful I didn't make an even bigger mistake by accepting his proposal."

"Do you really think so?" he asked.

She nodded, needing to believe it was true, needing to believe that she hadn't hurt Rowan without good reason. Especially when she'd ripped her own heart out in the process.

Marcus went directly to *La Noticia* and used his not-insubstantial powers of persuasion to convince Alex Girard to shelve the scandalous story in exchange for an exclusive interview with the prince regent and his fiancée once the engagement was officially announced. The reporter, recognizing the value of establishing goodwill with a member of the royal family, agreed.

Afterward Marcus went to visit Elena Leandres. Though the reporter's responses to his questions had been carefully worded to protect the identification of his source, there had been enough clues in what he did say for Marcus to recognize his aunt's hand in things.

The princess royal wasn't nearly as reasonable as Girard.

"There are other papers," she told Marcus upon learning that the story of Rowan's affair with Lara had been shelved. "Maybe not as reputable as *La Noticia,* but more than happy to give me the headlines I want."

"I don't doubt that's true. Just as I don't doubt that they'd also be happy to print the story about your attempts to discredit Rowan by paying Chantal St. Laurent to seduce him. Or an interview with the prostitute in Manilla who claims to be carrying Cameron's child."

"It's not his," she snapped.

"No—and you had the DNA test done to prove it, didn't you? Which means you couldn't have been sure." Marcus held her gaze for a long moment. "You want to play dirty, Princess? Go ahead. Just be forewarned that I will do anything to protect my family."

She shot him a glare filled with pure hatred.

Marcus took that to mean his aunt would back off—at least for now—and he walked out of her apartment, satisfied that he'd accomplished his task.

Lara finalized the details for her trip to Ireland with the children, then ensured she had a letter of permission from Rowan—delivered through his secretary—along with the children's passports. She hadn't expected that he would really try to prevent her from leaving the country, nor had she expected that she wouldn't see him at all in the ten days that had passed since he'd proposed to her in the rose garden.

By some twist of fate that she chose not to question, Girard seemed to have lost interest in publicizing the rumor that she'd been involved with the prince. Still, she believed she was doing the right thing in going away—she needed some space and time to let her heart begin to heal.

She was completing a last-minute check of the children's rooms to ensure they hadn't forgotten anything that was crucial to getting through the next few weeks— Damon's stuffed monkey, Lexi's favorite doll, Christian's books—when the summons came from Prince Rowan.

Ten minutes, she thought as she picked up the suitcase she'd returned to her own room to retrieve, and she would have been in the back of the limo with the children and on her way to the airport. Instead she was on her way to Rowan's office to see the man who—even if he didn't know it—held her heart in the palm of his hand.

"You wanted to see me, Your Highness?"

"Yes, Miss Brennan." But he finished signing the paperwork on his desk and waited for his secretary to leave before he even looked up. "I saw the chauffeur loading suitcases into the car. Were you planning to leave without a word?"

She swallowed. "I told the children to say goodbye."

"They did," he told her. "I wondered if you were going to."

"I thought we'd said everything we needed to say in the garden the other day." Her chin tipped up just a fraction. "And I took Lady Barrow's presence here last evening to mean that you agreed."

Rowan noted the hint of irritation in Lara's tone, filed it. And he didn't tell her that Lady Victoria had come to the palace without an invitation, or that he'd made it clear that he had no intention of marrying her before he sent her on her way again.

He did push his chair back and walk around his desk,

so that he was facing her without any barriers between them, though not so close that he could touch her. "Then you assumed wrong."

Her hands were linked in front of her, held together so tightly her knuckles were white. "I really need to be going. We're scheduled to leave in less than an hour."

"That plane isn't going anywhere until I say so." He wasn't in the habit of using his power arbitrarily, but he couldn't deny that there were times when he was glad he could do so.

Her jaw set. "What do you want from me, Rowan?"

"The truth," he said. "I told you the other day that I love you. Maybe I didn't choose the right time or place for that declaration, but poor planning doesn't make the feelings any less real."

She dropped her gaze. "Candlelight and soft music wouldn't have changed anything."

"Because you don't love me."

She nodded.

"I want to hear you say it, Lara."

She swallowed, but then she lifted her gaze and locked her eyes with his. "I don't love you."

But the defiance in her tone and the sparks in her eyes told a different story. He nodded, as if satisfied by her response. "Then it probably won't matter to you that I got a phone call yesterday from Alex Girard," he said casually.

He saw the uncertainty now, the flicker of wariness, and knew that she was remembering the day that she'd tried to tell him about the reporter. He hadn't remembered himself until the man started talking, asking for confirmation of the exclusive interview Marcus had promised in exchange for axing the story about the prince's affair with the nanny.

"It doesn't change anything," she said again.

"Not if you won't let it."

"We come from different backgrounds. We live in different worlds, Rowan. You have to know that a relationship between us would never work."

But she wanted to believe it could—he saw that now, the wary hope, the fear, the confusion. She *did* love him, but she didn't believe *she* was worthy of *his* love. The seeds of her insecurities had been planted too deep to be easily uprooted.

Rowan didn't need it to be easy. He would do whatever was necessary to prove to her that he did love her, and he would trust that her feelings for him would win out, that she would be willing to take a chance on love—for both of them.

"I don't happen to agree, but that's your call," he said, understanding that he couldn't make that decision for her. "Enjoy your trip, Lara."

"Thank you," she murmured.

No, he couldn't make the decision for her, but he was going to do everything in his power to help her decide in his favor. He followed her to the door, as if he was only intending to see her out, but it was really only a ploy to move closer to her. "Oh, there was one more thing before you go."

She looked at him warily, as if realizing she was trapped. "What's that?"

"This," he said, and lowered his mouth to hers.

It was more than a kiss—it was a promise of the love that filled his heart.

She held herself still for a moment, then—on a sigh that spoke as much of frustration as acceptance—her lips softened and finally responded. Her arms came around him, her body yielded, and then she was kissing him back with a passion he knew she'd never felt for anyone else. He savored the moment, the connection that had always been there between them, and the hope that he hadn't lost her completely.

He could have pushed for more. She would have given more. And then she would have withdrawn even further. She'd been hurt too many times to give her heart easily— by the father she'd never known, the mother who never wanted her and, though he hated to admit it, by him.

He couldn't blame her for being wary. He could only hope that with time, she would come to accept his feelings and acknowledge her own. And the time he gave her would allow him to put his plan into action.

It was this thought that helped him ease away when he wanted only to sink deeper into her.

"I'll see you in three weeks," he said, and somehow managed to smile as she walked out the door with both his future and his heart in her hands.

Chapter Thirteen

Christian spent most of the flight reading; Lexi watched a movie; Damon slept; and Lara tried not to think about Rowan's goodbye kiss—and the way she'd kissed him back. He'd caught her off guard, or at least that was the reasoning she used to justify her response, even if the justification was only in her own mind.

She hadn't struggled. How could she fight against something she wanted so desperately? Instead she'd savored every moment, memorized every detail, accepting it for what it was—a final kiss goodbye. She'd wrapped her arms around him, pressed her body close to his and told him with her actions the words she didn't dare speak aloud.

When he'd finally ended the kiss, her throat was tight, her knees were quivering, and her heart was breaking all over again. He'd held her for another moment, though, those dark chocolate eyes seeing far more than she wanted him to. Then he rubbed his thumb gently over her bottom lip, moist and swollen from his kiss, and said, "I'll see you in three weeks."

She was no longer certain that three weeks would be enough time to get over him.

She leaned her head back in her seat and closed her eyes against the tears that threatened. Though Tesoro del Mar had become her home in so many ways over the past few years, she enjoyed her frequent visits to Ireland with the children. But now, with every mile that passed, she was conscious not of what she was going toward but who she was leaving behind—the man she loved.

Maybe a few weeks with family was just what she needed to help her remember where she'd come from, remind her of the distance between herself and the prince and all the reasons their lives wouldn't mesh. By the time she returned to Tesoro del Mar at the end of the three weeks, she expected that the prince's engagement would have been announced and he would be deep in the midst of wedding plans.

Then she would have no choice but to get over him and get on with her life.

Rowan planned to give Lara a week—long enough to realize she missed him but not too long to worry that he'd forgotten about her. He made it to day five before he decided he was probably suffering more than she was, and he called his brothers together for a family meeting.

Marcus, despite having no interest in settling down with one woman anytime soon, proceeded to offer both unwanted and unnecessary advice. Eric, always more comfortable with his duties at sea than those required of him by the palace, nevertheless hadn't hesitated to come back when asked by his brother and had been much more quietly supportive. In the end, all that mattered to Rowan was that he could count on both of them.

He hadn't spoken to Lara at all since he'd been gone, but he'd been in touch with Maeve and Brian Seward, the children's grandparents. He knew they were planning to head up to their summer cottage soon and that Lara was spending a few days with David Mitchell in Kilmore before making the journey to the lake with them. Rowan was determined to put his plan into action before then.

With that thought in mind, he called Lionel into his office and said, "I'd like you to arrange a press conference."

"Of course, sir."

"Tomorrow afternoon. You know my schedule better than I do, so set it up whenever I have a free hour."

"May I let the media know what it is regarding?"

Rowan smiled. "It's an update on my wedding plans."

When Lara thought of family, even before she thought of the mother who had given birth to her, she thought of Stephanie and David. The Mitchells had taken a shy, scared child into their hearts and home and changed her life. Over the years, Lara had acknowledged and accepted the fact that her mother hadn't ever wanted her, but through some extraordinary stroke of luck, Stephanie and David had.

When her mother died, Lara had been more frightened and confused than grief-stricken by the loss. When Stephanie passed away, after a long and torturous battle with ALS, Lara had been devastated. She'd returned for the funeral and taken an additional two weeks off to spend with David, worried that he wouldn't be able to cope with the loss of the woman he'd loved for most of his life.

Eighteen months had passed since that last trip home, and as eager as Lara had been to get away from the palace and the ongoing preparations for Rowan's wedding, she was just as eager to see David again.

When she called to tell him she was in town, he invited her for dinner.

"It's from the frozen-food section of the supermarket," he apologized as he removed the tray of lasagna out of the oven.

"I came for the company, not the food," she assured him, though she knew they were both thinking about Stephanie and the wonderful home-cooked meals she always used to put on the table.

Lara dished up the pasta while David uncorked a bottle of wine, then they carried their plates and glasses to the table.

"How long are you visiting this time?" he asked.

"Only a few days. The Sewards want to take the kids up to the lake and, of course, I'll go with them."

"How are the children coping?"

"The first couple of months were really hard, but they're doing better now."

"It's so hard to lose someone you love," he murmured. "Especially when that someone is the center of your world."

She reached across the table to squeeze his hand. "How are *you* coping?"

"The first couple of months were really hard," he echoed her words.

"But you're doing better now?"

He managed to smile for her. "Yes, I am."

They ate in companionable silence for several minutes before Lara broached the topic that had been nagging at the back of her mind since she'd taken the call from that tabloid reporter. Actually, it was a question that had nagged at her for years, though she'd managed to ignore it most of the time, not certain she was prepared for the truth. But now she found herself not just wanting but needing answers. She might not be worthy of a prince, but she had to know who she was and where she came from.

"I remember Stephanie telling me that she and my mom were friends, as well as second cousins."

David nodded. "Very good friends at one time."

"The kind of friends who shared their deepest secrets?"

He hesitated, then asked, "What is it you really want to know, Lara?"

She traced the base of her wineglass with a fingertip. "I just can't help wondering if maybe she knew—or at least suspected—who my father is."

He laid his fork and knife down, pushed his plate aside. "Yes, Stephanie had some suspicions."

"Did she share them with you?"

His smile was wry. "The subject of your paternity was something we discussed at great length before we went to America to bring you home."

"Then you do know?"

"She wanted to tell you, but she was waiting for you to ask. She wanted to be sure you were ready to know. When she was dying—" he glanced away, but not before she saw the dampness in his eyes "—she asked me to tell you. I probably should have done so before now, but it wasn't something I wanted to dump on you right after the funeral and it's not the type of conversation to have on the telephone."

She picked up her glass of wine, sipped.

"When Felicia first told us about her baby, she claimed that I was the father."

Lara bobbled her glass, sloshing cabernet sauvignon over the rim and onto the antique lace tablecloth. She jumped up and ran to the kitchen for a cloth to wipe up the spill. But her efforts at removing the stain only seemed to help it spread.

David's hand covered hers, halting her frantic scrubbing. "Leave it."

She shook her head, her eyes blurred with tears. "I can't. This is Stephanie's favorite—"

"Lara." His tone was gentle but firm. "You wanted to know—give me a chance to tell you."

She looked up at him, as if she was seeing him for the first time. This man that she'd often thought of as a father. Was it really possible—could he *be* her father?

She sank back into her chair. "Is it…true?"

He gave a slight shake of his head. "No."

She let out a breath, uncertain if she was relieved or disappointed. "Then why would my mother say something like that?"

"Because it wasn't outside the realm of possibility."

She couldn't hide her shock. "You had an affair with my mother?"

"Very briefly, but yes." His hand wasn't quite steady when he lifted his glass to his lips. "I gave her the money to go to America."

"To hide what you thought was your bastard child."

He winced at the harshness of her words, but didn't deny the accusation. "I'm not proud of my actions—or my weakness. Felicia used me and lied to me, but I made it possible. I failed to turn her away when I should have, then did turn her away when she needed my help."

She should have left the past in the past. But now that she'd started to dig for the answers, she found herself with even more questions. "Were you married to Stephanie at the time?"

He nodded. "We'd been trying to have a baby of our own. After several early-term miscarriages, she finally had a pregnancy that went into its second term. After she passed the six-month mark, we got really excited—planning in earnest for the baby. But there were unexpected complications when she went into labor, and the baby died."

Even after so many years, she heard the grief in his voice and knew he still mourned the baby he and Stephanie had lost. Though her heart couldn't help but ache for what they'd been through, she couldn't let her empathy distract her from finally getting the truth he'd promised her.

"What does that have to do with you and my mother?"

"Steph went through a really tough time after we lost the baby. She was withdrawn and depressed, and every time I tried to reach her, she turned me away. Not just physically but emotionally. I felt so alone, grieving for the child we'd lost and terrified of losing the woman I loved."

"And Felicia offered you comfort." Lara might have been too young at the time to understand what was happening, but she'd seen her mother in action. And though she wasn't ready to absolve David of all responsibility, she'd never met a man who could turn her mother away once she'd set her sights on him.

"Yes," he said simply.

"Did Stephanie know?"

"I couldn't lie to her—which wasn't something Felicia anticipated. She came back a few weeks later, told me she was pregnant and threatened to tell Stephanie if I didn't give her money to go to America."

"But you gave her the money anyway."

"I'd told Stephanie about the affair, but I didn't want her to know about the pregnancy. She'd just lost our baby—I didn't know how she'd react to the news of another woman carrying my child."

"If you were so anxious to hide the evidence of your affair, why did you bring me back here?"

"After Felicia died, I thought—I hoped—I would finally have the chance to be a father to a child who desperately needed one."

"And Stephanie was okay with that?"

"As soon as Stephanie knew about you, there was never any question about you coming to live with us. She'd long given up being angry. And you were an innocent child, and she wished only that you had truly been ours."

Lara felt her throat tighten because she knew it was true. Stephanie had tried so hard to ease her transition to a new country, to make her feel comfortable in her new family, and she'd always loved her unconditionally.

"Except that you weren't a child anymore when you came to us," David continued. "You were practically a young woman, more wary and distrustful than anyone your age should be, and desperately searching for your place in the world."

"When did you find out I wasn't your child?"

"Even before we brought you home. We were sorting through your mother's things to decide what to keep for you and found a copy of your birth certificate. I was with your mother in June, you were born in November."

"Then you couldn't possibly be my father."

He shook his head. "No. But Stephanie insisted on a paternity test—I don't know whether she thought the affair had been going on longer than I'd admitted to or if she believed you might have been born prematurely. And the interesting thing is, when the DNA results came back, they proved that I wasn't your father but that we did share some genetic markers."

"I don't understand."

"Neither did I, at first," he admitted. "Then I remembered that my brother, Derek, was killed in a car accident around the same time that Stephanie lost the baby."

"You think he might have been my father?"

David nodded. "We knew it was possible, but we weren't certain until we got the letters.

"It was just a few years ago," he explained. "Shortly after you moved to Tesoro del Mar, we received a package from Family Services in America. Apparently, in the process of relocating their offices, they'd sorted through old files and found some papers that had belonged to your mother. In those papers were some letters that Derek had written to her."

David pushed away from the table. "Let me get them for you."

He cleared away their dishes while she read the letters. There were only three and Derek wasn't a man of many words so it didn't take her long, but her throat was tight when she was done.

"All this time, I thought—*my mother told me*—my father didn't want me."

"Derek probably panicked when Felicia told him she was pregnant. He was young, a little reckless, more than a little irresponsible. But I also believe, had he not been killed, he would have done the right thing. He would have married your mother and been a father to you. But he never had the chance."

She swallowed. "And so she seduced you and tried to pass his baby off as yours."

"None of which she could have done without my complicity."

"But she lied—to me, to you, to Stephanie." She shook her head, angered and appalled by her mother's actions, by the deceptions that had hurt so many.

"She must have had her reasons."

"You've forgiven her," she realized.

"She gave far more than she took away when she brought you into our lives."

Lara held up the slim package of letters. "Can I keep these?"

"They are yours. I was just holding on to them for you." He smiled. "Like any good uncle would do."

Before she could get her mind around that, never mind respond to it, her cell phone signaled a text message had been received. It was Tanis's number, and the message was brief.

TURN ON TV. NOW.

"What's wrong?" David asked.

"I don't know." She frowned, wondering about the sense of urgency in her friend's message. "Tanis wants me to turn on the television."

"Then we should move into the other room."

She picked up the remote, scrolling through the channels until she found the report that had caught her friend's attention.

"Isn't that your prince?" David asked.

She knew that he used the term *your* to distinguish Rowan from British royalty, but she couldn't help remembering that, for a very brief time, he had been hers, and she had been his.

"It's Prince Rowan," she agreed. And though her heart ached to look at the man she loved but couldn't have, she was unable to tear her gaze away from the screen.

"Turn it up," David urged. "I can't hear what he's saying."

Though Lara didn't really want to hear the announcement of Rowan's engagement, she tapped the volume button.

"...the laws of Tesoro del Mar require that I marry within six months of my thirty-fifth birthday," Rowan was saying. "Not wanting to disappoint the good citizens of this country, I have been actively seeking a bride. I didn't expect to fall in love. In fact, had you asked me six months ago, I would have insisted I didn't want to fall in love. But somehow that's what happened."

The prince paused to smile as the crowd applauded his announcement with enthusiasm. As the applause slowly faded, questions could be heard from the reporters.

"What's her name?"

"Where is she?"

"Have you set a date for the wedding?"

Lara felt her stomach twist into knots as Rowan held up a hand for silence.

"I should get those dishes washed up." She started to turn away.

"Her name," Rowan said, "is Lara Brennan."

Chapter Fourteen

Lara felt David's gaze on her as she sank down onto the footstool, her own eyes riveted back to the television.

"You're going to marry the royal nanny?" one of the reporters asked, doubt etched in her voice.

"That's my plan," the prince responded. "But Miss Brennan's been a little resistant to the idea."

"Are you saying that she turned down your proposal?"

"The laws of Tesoro del Mar are very specific about who a royal might marry. As Miss Brennan doesn't fit the usual requirements, she encouraged me to choose a bride who did. The problem with that, of course, is that I only want Lara."

She couldn't believe he'd said it—during a televised press conference that was probably bouncing from satellite to satellite around the world. This was exactly what she'd been trying to avoid, and yet, maybe exactly what her heart needed.

"Are you planning to forfeit the throne? Or do you think you can circumvent the requirements of the law?"

"Thanks to my brother, Marcus, I have recently become aware of a legislative provision that would allow me to marry the woman I love."

The crowd was silent now, hanging on his every word.

"My family is supportive of my wish to make Lara my wife," he told them. "Both of my brothers believe she will be a princess Tesoro del Mar can be proud of. Prince Christian, Princess Alexandria and Prince Damon absolutely love her, and the staff of the royal household stand behind my decision. But I need the support of the people.

"I need all of you—all of the people of Tesoro del Mar—to vote 'yes' in a national referendum asking for the approval of Lara Brennan as my bride. Without your vote, I'm not sure I can convince her to marry me."

He found the camera and stared into it, and though she knew it was ridiculous, Lara felt as if he was looking right at her, speaking directly to her. And her heart pounded hard inside her chest, responding with a plea of its own. A plea to say yes, to accept what she so desperately wanted. But her head continued to resist, convinced that he didn't fully understand the consequences to the throne if the referendum failed.

As if he knew exactly what she was thinking, Rowan continued, "The only thing I know for sure is that if I can't be prince regent and have Lara as my wife, then I will give up my position. Because I won't give up on her."

"Does she love you?"

One side of his mouth kicked up in a half smile in response to the reporter's question. "I can only hope that she does, because I'm going to feel like a royal idiot otherwise."

Laughter rippled through the crowds, another question was asked, this one inquiring about the specific provisions of the legislation, and as Rowan began to respond, the local broadcast cut away.

"There you have it," the perky news anchor told her viewers. "After months of public speculation, Prince Rowan has finally made an announcement about his intention to take a bride. The only question now is, will Lara Brennan take *him?*"

The phone started ringing immediately after the broadcast. Some of the calls were from friends and neighbors who wanted to know if it was really true that Prince Rowan had proposed to Lara; more of the calls were from various media wanting her reaction to the prince's press conference. David ended up taking the phone off the hook so that he could get the real story from her, which she managed to spill along with more than a few tears.

"You're in love with him," David said, not questioning the fact.

"More than I ever thought I could love anyone," Lara admitted.

The man who had been a surrogate father and friend for so long and only recently an uncle, smiled. "Then why the heck didn't you say 'yes' when he asked you to marry him?"

She sighed. "Because this is exactly the situation that I was hoping to avoid. I know Rowan wants to believe that the citizens of Tesoro del Mar will support him, but what if they don't? What if they can't stand the thought of their prince marrying an illegitimate, untitled commoner. And a foreigner, no less?"

"You're an incredible woman and any man—even a prince—would be lucky to have you," David said loyally.

Lara managed to smile at that, but when she thought of

what might happen, the smile faded and her eyes filled with tears again. "He could lose the throne."

"He seems well aware of the risk he's taking," David assured her. "And more than willing to take that risk because he knows you're worth it. Now you need to realize it, too."

The referendum was set for July 9, two weeks after his press conference. During that time, the story of the prince's public proposal remained a hot topic in the media, but Lara didn't hear from Rowan at all. She tried not to let the media attention wear on her, certain that once the results of the referendum were in, the fervor would fade.

But with each day that passed without any word from Rowan, her own trepidation grew. She kept herself busy at the lake with the children and tried not to be conscious of every passing minute of every hour.

Finally it was referendum day. The polls opened, the polls closed, the ballots were counted. But the results were given only to Prince Rowan, for him to reveal to the people presumably after he shared them with the woman he hoped to marry. Still he didn't make any effort to contact her, and Lara found herself wondering if somewhere along the way he had changed his mind.

"He hasn't changed his mind," Tanis assured her after calling Lara to learn the results of the referendum—only to find out her friend didn't know.

"Then why hasn't he called?"

"Maybe he has laryngitis."

Lara tried to laugh, but it came out sounding more like a sob. "Or maybe the vote failed and he can't face the thought of losing everything that matters to him."

"You matter to him," Tan told her. "If you didn't, he wouldn't have put everything else on the line."

She hoped her friend was right, though there was part of her that feared the prince was, even now, with Lady Victoria Barrow, begging the other woman to forgive him for being a fool and asking her to be his wife.

"I should let you go," Tanis said, "because he's probably trying to call with the good news right now. I just have one more thing to say first."

"What's that?"

"No pink ruffles for me, either."

Lara managed to laugh as she said goodbye to her friend. Then she turned to place the phone back in its cradle and saw Rowan standing in the doorway.

Her heart leaped, her breath caught, and when she finally managed to speak, his name was barely a whisper from her lips.

"Rowan."

"Hello, Lara."

She couldn't believe it. He was here. Standing in front of her. In the flesh—and as breathtakingly handsome as always.

"I didn't know— Did you tell anyone you were coming?"

"I spoke to Brian before I flew out…to make sure you were still here."

"He didn't tell me you'd called."

"I asked him not to. I wanted to surprise you." His lips curved just a little. "Or maybe I wanted to make sure you didn't have a chance to run again."

"I was trying to save you—from yourself."

He smiled a real smile this time, tender and warm and just for her. "You did save me," he told her. "The minute you walked into my life. It just took me a while to realize it."

"And the vote?" she prompted, not wanting him to see

how effectively he was seducing her with nothing more than the heat in his eyes and the soft cadence of his voice.

He moved closer now, close enough to touch her. And he did. He cradled her face in his hands, his thumbs brushing over her cheeks in a feather-soft caress that made her tremble and yearn. She forgot that he had yet to answer her question as his head dipped toward her and her eyes drifted shut. But he didn't kiss her. At least not the way she expected he would, not the way she needed him to.

There was no fiery heat or stormy passion but simple tenderness in the touch of his lips to her brow, then her eyelids—first one then the other, the tip of her nose and finally her lips.

It had been weeks since she'd been in his arms, a seeming eternity since she'd felt the press of his body against hers, the pounding of his heart in rhythm with hers. It was as glorious as she remembered and somehow, so much more.

When he ended their kiss, her mind was misty with hopes and dreams, and it was several minutes more before they finally cleared away and she remembered the question she'd asked.

"The vote," she said again.

"Does it matter?"

She could only stare at him. "How can you even ask that question? Of course it matters."

"I love you, Lara. *That* is what matters."

"Tell me," she demanded.

"Do you love me?"

She dropped her head against his chest, shaking it from side to side in frustration. "Would I be agonizing over this if I didn't?"

"I wouldn't have thought so," he admitted, amusement

evident in his tone. "But I'd kind of like to hear you say the words, anyway."

She tipped her head back. "I love you, Rowan, but if you tell me that you lost the vote, I'm going to kill you."

"Then my life is safe—and I'm trusting it will also be blissfully happy with you by my side."

"They voted yes?"

He smiled and nodded.

"And you really want to marry me?"

"I really want to marry you," he said. "And not because I need to get married to secure the throne, but because I love you so much more than I ever thought I would love anyone.

"I'm not trying to change your life—I'm only asking you to share mine. I'm asking you to be my wife and my partner, to be part of the family that includes my brother's children and any that we might have together, to go to sleep beside me at night, wake up with me in the morning and love me forever.

"Now, in case all of that wasn't specific enough, I'm going to ask just one more time." And then he did something she'd never expected—he got down on one knee. "Lara Brennan, will you marry me?"

She could hardly speak, her throat was so clogged with emotion, so she nodded.

He shook his head. "I've proposed to you twice now, put my heart on the line in front of the whole world. I want to hear you actually say 'yes'."

"Yes," she finally said. "Yes, I will marry you."

This time when he kissed her, there was fire and passion and an almost desperate need to be together after so long apart.

He tore his mouth from hers to ask, "Where are the kids?"

"They went to a music festival in town with their grandparents." She yanked his shirt out of his pants. "They won't be home until late."

"Gracias, Dio," he said.

Then he was kissing her again.

He had her blouse undone and was reaching for the button of her pants when his hands suddenly froze. "Wait."

"Wait?" She was sure she would explode if he wasn't inside her in about thirty seconds. "You've got to be kidding."

He pulled away from her, digging into his pocket. "I have a ring. I can't believe I forgot the ring."

"I can wait until later for the ring," she assured him.

He pulled out the small velvet box. "I can't. Throughout the flight, all I could think about was putting this ring on your finger and making love to you while you were wearing nothing else but the symbol of our promise to each other."

The words—and the heartfelt emotion in them—had her tearing up again. Then he flipped open the lid and the tears spilled over.

"It's a natural yellow topaz. Fifteen carats, circled by three rows of round pavé set diamonds. It reminded me of the earrings you were wearing the first night we made love—and of you."

"It's stunning."

He took the ring from the box, slid it onto her finger.

"And heavy."

"That's so you'll never forget you're wearing it," he told her. And now that it was on her finger, he made quick work of getting her naked, then helped her strip away the last of his clothes and lowered her to the bed. "So you'll never forget you're mine."

"And you're mine." She wrapped her arms around him, drew him down with her. *"Mi amor está por siempre."*

"As my love for you is forever," he told her.

Epilogue

Prince Regent Weds Royal Nanny
by Alex Girard

It was the wedding that many thought would never happen.

For those who had an invitation to witness the marriage of Prince Rowan Santiago and Lara Brennan at the Cathedral of Christ the King, it was a momentous occasion that will not soon be forgotten.

The bride wore a custom-made taffeta gown and carried a cascading bouquet of lilies as she walked down the aisle on the arm of her uncle, David Mitchell. She was attended to by longtime friend Tanis Rowlands, with Princess Alexandria as her flower girl and Prince Damon carrying the rings.

The groom was in military uniform bearing his rank and royal insignia. He was joined at the altar by younger brothers, Prince Eric and Prince Marcus, along with his eldest nephew, Prince Christian.

The couple exchanged their vows before approximately three hundred guests, then made a brief appearance on the front steps of the church where they were presented to the crowd as Their Royal Highnesses Prince Rowan and Princess Lara of Tesoro del Mar.

The thirty-five-year-old prince regent might have succumbed to the pressures of tradition and Parliament when he set the date for his wedding six months ago, but if there is anyone in the country who still has doubts about the genuineness of his affection for his bride, he didn't see the kiss the prince planted on the lips of his new princess in front of the church yesterday afternoon.

There was enough spark and sizzle in the air after the passionate embrace to convince even the biggest skeptic that this royal wedding will lead to a very happily ever after.

* * * * *

Mills & Boon® Special Moments
brings you a sneak preview…

In Family in Progress *restoring classic cars is
widowed dad Steven's passion. And when
magazine photographer Samara Kenzo shows up
to snap his masterpieces, her focus is squarely on
the handsome mechanic. But can Samara and
Steven's little girl learn to get along?*

*Turn the page for a peek at this
fantastic new story from Brenda Harlen,
available next month in
Mills & Boon® Special Moments!*

Family in Progress

by

Brenda Harlen

Life was much simpler for Steven Warren when he worked at Al's Body Shop, when someone else was in charge and he simply did what he was told to do. But a man couldn't work twelve- and fourteen-hour days when he had children at home who needed him, which was why the offer to work at *Classic* magazine in Chicago had been as welcome as it was unexpected.

Steven had long had a passion for classic cars, and the opportunity to work for the magazine, finding vehicles in need of restoration and leading the team through that process, was one he couldn't pass up.

And if Steven sometimes felt out of his element now that he spent more time in an office than in a garage, he figured the opportunity to make a desperately needed new start with his family was more than adequate compensation.

But now he felt trapped between the proverbial rock and hard place. He'd been entrusted with the responsibility of hiring a new features photographer for the magazine and he was determined to find the perfect person for the job. Except that—on the basis of the applications he'd received in response to his ad—the perfect person had yet to apply and he was running out of time.

And then, just last week, his sister-in-law sent him an e-mail that offered a solution to his dilemma. Or so he hoped.

He found a bottle of Tylenol in his desk and shook a couple of pills out of the bottle to ward off the headache that had been lurking behind his eyes since breakfast.

The morning had not got off to a great start. His twelve-year-old daughter had been in a mood—again. It seemed Caitlin had given him nothing but attitude since they'd moved to Chicago at the end of the summer.

He wondered if she would ever understand that he'd done it *for* her and not to spite her. Since her mother's death almost three years earlier, Caitlin had fallen in with a questionable crowd and Steven hadn't known how to tear his daughter away from their negative influence. So he'd uprooted his fractured family and moved them to Illinois.

He swallowed the pills with a mouthful of lukewarm coffee and scanned his sister-in-law's e-mail once again.

Hi Steven,

Richard told me that you're looking for a new photographer—someone who can breathe new life into the magazine—and it just so happens that I have a friend who would be perfect for the job. Her name is Samara Kenzo. We went to college together then were coworkers and roommates in Tokyo before I married your brother.

Anyway, Samara has recently moved to Chicago and is looking for work. I'm not asking you to hire her, of course, just to meet with her. (Though I'm sure you'll agree that she's exactly what you need once you've had a chance to interview her and look at her portfolio!) I suggested that she drop off a résumé at your office so that you can contact her directly if you think she might be a suitable candidate.

Thanks,

Jenny

PS. Don't forget about the dinner party we're having on the fourth. It's been far too long since we've seen you and I won't accept any excuses this time :)

Steven winced as he read the last line, He'd been making a lot of excuses to avoid spending time with his brother and sister-in-law over the past few months. Richard was the only brother he had and he'd liked Jenny from their first meeting, but seeing them together was just too painful a reminder of everything he'd lost.

The buzz of the phone interrupted his melancholic thoughts. He closed his e-mail as he picked up the receiver. "Yes?"

"There's a Samara Kenzo here to see you," his assistant told him.

"Thanks, Carrie." He was both excited and wary about meeting his sister-in-law's friend. Excited because the résumé she'd dropped off was more than impressive, and wary because he knew that if the interview went well, he'd have to attend that dinner party—if for no other reason than to thank Jenny for the referral.

Samara Kenzo was uneasy even before she stepped into Steven Warren's office. Though she appreciated Jenny's confidence in her abilities and was aware of her own talent, she wasn't convinced her friend's brother-in-law would be impressed with her credentials. She'd taken a lot of pictures in the past six years and even won several awards for her work, but she had her doubts as to whether she belonged at a car magazine and she worried about how she might convince Jenny's brother-in-law of something she wasn't even sure of herself.

As she glanced around the space, she was even less sure, but she strode confidently across the room to shake his outstretched hand.

Steven hadn't come to Tokyo for his brother's wedding so she'd never had occasion to meet him before now, but he looked enough like Richard that she had no doubt of his identity.

Tall, dark and absolutely yummy.

She shoved that thought aside impatiently. She wanted this job. She did *not* want to feel the first stirrings of a physical attraction after more than two years of not feeling anything at all.

"Thank you for taking the time to meet with me, Mr. Warren."

"It's my pleasure," he responded politely.

"Is it?" she wondered.

He seemed startled by her response, and she smiled to soften the words as she handed her portfolio to him.

"I'm guessing that this interview is more in the nature of an obligation than a pleasure," she explained her question. "But I'm hoping that, by the time we're finished here, you'll be glad you took the time."

He considered her words as he thumbed through the pages of her portfolio, pausing once or twice but otherwise giving no hint of any reaction to the contents.

"Do you always say exactly what's on your mind?" he asked.

"Usually."

"And do you find that outspokenness an attribute or a detriment?"

"It can be both. But I've found that the best way to get what I want is to communicate what I want clearly." She met his gaze. "I want this job, Mr. Warren."

"Why *Classic*?" he asked. "What is it about this magazine that intrigues you?"

Samara knew she should have been prepared for that question and had an answer at the ready. But her tendency to speak her mind aside, she certainly couldn't tell him the truth about this—that she needed a job and this one seemed as good as any.

She didn't really care about cars—classic or otherwise. As far as she was concerned, they were just a means to an end, a form of transportation. But she could hardly tell *that* to the man whose office was decorated with framed photos of polished vehicles and who had every available surface covered with scale models of classic machines.

"I like a challenge," she said at last. "I've worked at several different jobs, taking pictures of everything from fashion models to fine cuisine, but I've never worked with the automotive industry. I thought this job would give me an opportunity to expand my—" she scrambled to find the right word in English "—horizontal."

Steven frowned, and she wondered what she'd said wrong. Then his eyes cleared and his lips curved slightly. "I think you mean 'horizons.'"

She shrugged. It wasn't the first time her grasp of the English language had slipped and she knew it wouldn't be the last.

"I also thought it would be a great opportunity for you," she told him.

He lifted a brow. "How so?"

"Because your magazine will benefit from my creative energy and enthusiasm."

He flipped through several more pages in her portfolio before he spoke again.

"You might be right," he agreed.

But then he stood and offered his hand, and her blossoming hope withered.

"Thank you for your time, Ms. Kenzo. I have some other applicants to interview, but I'll be in touch by the end of the week."

"Thank *you,* Mr. Warren." She forced a smile as she shook his hand. "I'll look forward to hearing from you."

And she left his office, resigned to checking the employment listings in the local newspaper when she got home.

But first, she was meeting Jenny for lunch.

SPECIAL MOMENTS 2-in-1

Coming next month

TRUSTING RYAN by Tara Taylor Quinn

When a case comes between sexy cop Ryan Mercedes
and his best friend Audrey Lincoln, can he learn to
see things her way?

THE BACHELOR'S STAND-IN WIFE by Susan Crosby

David Falcon needed a business-arrangement bride.
His new housekeeper seemed the ideal candidate,
until he started to fall for her…

HIS MIRACLE BABY by Karen Sandler

Shani had to know if Logan could be more than just the father
of her child – was he, perhaps, the man of her dreams?

RETURN TO EMMETT'S MILL by Kimberly Van Meter

Home at last, Tasha Simmons can't avoid the man she'd
hoped to marry. He hasn't forgotten their love. *Or* forgiven
her for leaving…

HIS SECRET PAST by Ellen Hartman

Anna Walsh may be the only chance he has to save his life's
work. But what she wants may be more than Mason can give…

A PLACE CALLED HOME by Margaret Watson

Zoe McInnes has stood up to the worst that life has thrown
at her. But when *worst* is sexy lawyer Gideon Tate,
life begins to get very exciting!

On sale 17ᵗʰ July 2009

Available at WHSmith, Tesco, ASDA, Eason and all good bookshops.
For full Mills & Boon range including eBooks visit
www.millsandboon.co.uk

SPECIAL MOMENTS

Single titles coming next month

TRUST A COWBOY
by Judy Christenberry

Rancher Pete Ledbetter needed a wife – fast! After a
summer romance he knew he was compatible with
chef Mary Jo Michaels. But winning back her trust
would be nearly impossible…

FAMILY IN PROGRESS
by Brenda Harlen

A romance with her sexy boss wasn't part of the deal –
until a date led to an amazing kiss! Samara suddenly
found she was falling for the wary widower and
his irresistible kids…

DIAMOND IN THE ROUGH
by Marie Ferrarella

Miranda was as protective of her heart as she was of her
family name – she didn't want some journalist digging
into their business. Mike's pursuit of the truth
could rob him of true love!

FALLING FOR THE LONE WOLF
by Crystal Green

Liam McCree was bad news for women. But Jenny's
warmth and spirit made him want more than just a fling.
Could these two opposites find a way to make
a life together?

On sale 17th July 2009

Available at WHSmith, Tesco, ASDA, Eason and all good bookshops.
For full Mills & Boon range including eBooks visit
www.millsandboon.co.uk

2 FREE

BOOKS AND A SURPRISE GIFT!

We would like to take this opportunity to thank you for reading this Mills & Boon® book by offering you the chance to take TWO more specially selected titles from the Special Edition series absolutely FREE! We're also making this offer to introduce you to the benefits of the Mills & Boon® Book Club™—

- ★ FREE home delivery
- ★ FREE gifts and competitions
- ★ FREE monthly Newsletter
- ★ Exclusive Mills & Boon Book Club offers
- ★ Books available before they're in the shops

Accepting these FREE books and gift places you under no obligation to buy, you may cancel at any time, even after receiving your free shipment. Simply complete your details below and return the entire page to the address below. You don't even need a stamp!

YES! Please send me 2 free Special Edition books and a surprise gift. I understand that unless you hear from me, I will receive 4 superb new titles every month for just £3.19 each, postage and packing free. I am under no obligation to purchase any books and may cancel my subscription at any time. The free books and gift will be mine to keep in any case.

E9ZED

Ms/Mrs/Miss/Mr ....Initials ....

BLOCK CAPITALS PLEASE

Surname ....

Address ....

....

....Postcode..

Send this whole page to:
UK: FREEPOST CN81, Croydon, CR9 3WZ

Offer valid in UK only and is not available to current Mills & Boon Book Club subscribers to this series. Overseas and Eire please write for details and readers in Southern Africa write to Box 3010, Pinegowie, 2123 RSA. We reserve the right to refuse an application and applicants must be aged 18 years or over. Only one application per household. Terms and prices subject to change without notice. Offer expires 30th September 2009. As a result of this application, you may receive offers from Harlequin Mills & Boon and other carefully selected companies. If you would prefer not to share in this opportunity please write to The Data Manager, PO Box 676, Richmond, TW9 1WU.

Mills & Boon® is a registered trademark owned by Harlequin Mills & Boon Limited.
The Mills & Boon® Book Club™ is being used as a trademark.